IRISH ANIMAL
FOLK TALES
FOR CHILDREN

DOREEN MCBRIDE

The History Press

*This book is dedicated to my dear friend Dr Joy Higginson,
who has been a constant source of encouragement – although
as a past headmistress of Victoria College, Belfast, she really
should know better – and to my special friends, Alfie (eight),
Cadan (five), Chris (thirteen) and Louis (seven).*

Illustrated by the author
Cover illustration by Su Eaton

WARNING: This book is
not suitable for adults.

First published 2021

The History Press
The Mill, Brimscombe Port
Stroud, Gloucestershire, GL5 2QG
www.thehistorypress.co.uk

© Doreen McBride, 2021

The right of Doreen McBride to be identified as the Author
of this work has been asserted in accordance with the
Copyright, Designs and Patents Act 1988.

British Library Cataloguing in Publication Data.
A catalogue record for this book is available from the British Library.

ISBN 978 0 7509 9372 2

Typesetting and origination by Typo•glyphix, Burton-on-Trent
Printed in Great Britain by TJ Books Limited, Padstow, Cornwall.

CONTENTS

INTRODUCTION

Did you ever feel so scared you could poop your pants? Well, that's how I feel now! I love animals and I love folk tales, so I thought, 'Why don't I write a book about animals in folk tales?'

The trouble is I don't really know what a folk tale is or what an animal is.

I know a folk tale's a very old story that's been passed down from one generation to the next. But how old is old?

I know a 'once upon a time' sort of time counts but what about fifty years old? How long does it take a story to become a folk tale?

The other thing that's scaring me is, if a person turns into an animal does he or she count as a person or an animal?

I asked my special friends Alfie and Louis and we decided that if I've heard a story from say, fifty years ago, and I like it, I should share it. If a person turns into an animal that person can be counted as an animal. I hope you'll forgive us if you disagree.

As I've said, I'm scared stiff but I've just remembered an old story about a scary giant who lived in the mountains above a valley and terrorised people living below. Every time people tried to escape the giant used to come out and shout:

Fee Fi Fo Fum,
I smell your bum!

And they all ran away! Then one day a very brave person decided to get out of the valley.

I'm sorry, I don't know if it was a boy or a girl – so let's say it was you in a past life! When you decided to escape you grabbed a sword and charged towards the giant. As you ran, the giant became smaller and smaller and smaller until you were standing in front of him and were able to pick him up in your hand and ask, 'What is your name?' He said, 'My name is Fear!'

Has that ever happened to you? You were scared of doing something, like having to read in Assembly, or sing a solo? Then you did it and were pleased with yourself. You faced your giant and it disappeared.

I think the best thing I can do is face my fear so I'm going to get on with writing. It's not as if writing stories is dangerous, in which case I'd be sensible and not do it. I don't want either you, or me, to be stupid and do something dangerous! That's a no-brainer.

1

TITANIC'S GHOSTLY DOGS

I've always been fascinated by *Titanic*. She was the largest, most beautiful ship in the whole wide world and she was built in Belfast.

My grandfather, Sam Finlay, was a cabinet maker, who worked on the first-class cabins. He said they were fantastic and he wished he had enough money to travel in one of them. (A first-class ticket for a suite on *Titanic* cost £870 – in today's money that would be £49,642!) The average working man's wage was £160 a year and he had to work a fifty-six-hour week to earn that! It's no wonder Grandpa said, 'Ye don't know you're living today!' (He died in 1963.)

Titanic was built by the famous White Star Line. On her first, and only, voyage she picked up crew and passengers in Southampton before sailing to Cherbourg, where other passengers embarked.

Titanic was built in Thompson Dry Dock in Belfast's Titanic Quarter. I climbed down the metal stairway to the bottom of the dock and felt I was surrounded by gigantic cliffs. I dandered along the bottom and an old man came and told me about the *Nomadic*.

He said, '*Titanic*'s first port of call was Cherbourg. Its harbour wasn't big enough for such a large ship so two small boats (tenders), *Nomadic* and *Traffic*, ferried people across.

'The *Nomadic* is one quarter of Titanic's size and she, like *Titanic*, was designed by Thomas Andrews and had similar luxurious finishes. The crew stretched a gangway between the *Nomadic*'s flying bridge and *Titanic*'s E Deck to enable passengers to board.'

The passengers included Miss Ann Elisabeth Isham with her beloved Great Dane, and one of the world's richest men, John Jacob Astor, his young wife Madeleine, and their dog, an Airedale called Kitty. (He had booked the most expensive cabin. Imagine that! Nearly £50,000, in today's money, for a one-way ticket to New York! If I spent £50,000 on a single ticket to cross the Atlantic I'd wet my knickers!)

The sea was very choppy so the gangway swayed like mad and several men did their best to hold it steady, but even so a woman fell and twisted her ankle. The Astors and their dog got across safely.

Kitty and the Great Dane weren't the only dogs on Titanic. There were twelve altogether, but only the tiny ones you could stick up your coat survived (two Pomeranians and a Pekinese called Sun Yat Sen.) She boarded at Cherbourg.

Titanic sailed from Cherbourg to Queenstown on Ireland's south coast. More passengers embarked at Queenstown and a few disembarked. Then *Titanic* set out on the long journey to New York.

(Queenstown's name has been changed to Cobh. It has an interesting Titanic Museum that's well worth a visit. I went to see it when I was staying in Cork. I enjoyed the train along the coast from Cork to Cobh.)

The chairman of the White Star Line, Joseph Bruce Ismay, was on board. He wanted to cross the Atlantic in record time so he and the captain, Edward James Smith, ignored all the radio messages about the danger of icebergs and sailed full steam ahead. On 12 April 1912 *Titanic* hit an iceberg and sank.

When *Nomadic*'s life at sea ended she was turned into a restaurant and moored on the River Seine beside the Eiffel Tower. Eventually she came up for auction. People in Belfast were very excited, so they decided to buy the old tender and bring her home. The Nomadic Preservation Society was formed and they worked very hard raising the money needed. They succeeded and now she's moored in Belfast's Hamilton Dock.

Poor *Nomadic* was in a very bad way when she arrived home! She'd had her top cut off so she could get under new bridges built over the River Seine after she'd been moored beside the Eiffel Tower, and some of her beautiful panelling had been removed. She was so rusty she was in danger of sinking and had to be tied to another ship to keep her afloat (they were towed by tugs).

When she got home, members of The *Nomadic* Preservation Society found some more of her panelling in a restaurant in Paris

Do you hear yon dog barking? Well it's not there!

and her lifeboats were in Belgium! They were brought home and restoration work began.

One night two men were working late in the *Nomadic*. It was dark. They heard voices, a man and a woman talking and dogs barking. There was nobody there! The men's hair stood on end and shivers shimmied up their spines. Ghosts!

Kitty, the Great Dane and their owners sank with the *Titanic*. Kitty's body was never found. John Jacob Astor's body was identified by the gold watch in his pocket. (His wife survived because he put her into a lifeboat.)

Miss Ann Elizabeth Isham got into a lifeboat, was not allowed to take her dog on board and climbed out again. Several days later her frozen body was recovered floating in the sea with her arms around her Great Dane.

I've no proof of this, but as John Jacob Astor was so fond of Kitty he probably went and got her out of *Titanic*'s kennels and went down with his dog. *Titanic* was lost, so he, Miss Ann Elizabeth Isham and their dogs have come back to haunt the *Nomadic* instead.

You can visit the *Nomadic*. She's moored in Belfast Lough beside the *Titanic* Museum. She's important because she's the last White Star Line ship anywhere in the world.

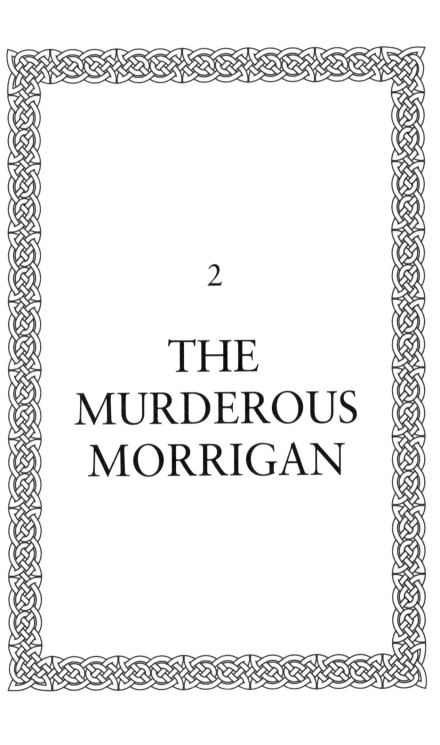

2

THE
MURDEROUS
MORRIGAN

This is a very old story, going back to the ancient people, called the Celts, who used to live in Ireland a long, long time ago, about 2,000 years ago. If you count time by the number of sleeps you could have had since this story was first told you'd have to count about 630,000 sleeps! You have to admit that's very old! It's been handed down hundreds of years.

The Morrigan was the Goddess of War. She had magic powers so she could change into any shape she liked! One minute she might be a cow, or a human, or a snake, or a wolf, or anything at all. Her 'proper' shape was a big black bird called a raven. It looks like a crow, but is much bigger. The Morrigan lived in Ravensdale – that's near Dundalk. There's a hamlet there today. You'll see it signposted on the main road between Dundalk and Newry.

One day the Morrigan was sitting on a tree in Ravensdale. She was bored and making bad-tempered 'Caw! Caw!' noises. She was a nasty bird, the kind of animal Ulster people call a 'bad baist' (beast).

Suddenly something caught her eye. She strained to see through the trees. What was it? Ahhhhhhhhhhhh! It was Cuculan. He was a Celt and I told you the Celts had a lot of peculiar habits. They loved to fight and wanted to get killed in battle because they thought their souls would go straight to a heaven called The Otherworld!

Before going into battle they took their clothes off and painted ferocious things, like animals, on their bodies in blue with a herb called 'woad'.

(In this climate I keep my clothes firmly on, although I can see being naked while fighting has advantages because you wouldn't make your mummy cross by getting your clothes covered in blood! It's hard to wash off!)

Cuculan was dressed for war! In other words, he was as naked as the day he was born and he'd painted his body blue!

'Wow!' thought the Morrigan, as she fell in love, 'OOOOOOOOOH! Wow! He's fit and he's dressed for war. I love a good fight!'

Wow! He's fit!

Ulster was in terrible danger because it was being attacked by Queen Maeve and her army, while the men of Ulster suffered from a terrible curse. Whenever Ulster was in danger, its warriors had terrible pains in their tummies so they couldn't get out of bed for nine days and nine nights.

Cuculan didn't suffer from the curse because he was the son of a god. He was all alone, defending Ulster.

Imagine that! How would you like to be alone fighting a whole army?

I wouldn't like it at all, but Cuculan was a champion fighter. My Granny was a great storyteller and she told me he could cut off 200 heads with one swipe of his sword! I didn't believe her so she said, 'Cuculan was the Champion of Ireland and a great hero and you never know what you can do until you try!'

That's true, isn't it? You don't know what you can do until you try but I don't suggest you try cutting anyone's head off.

Cuculan wasn't scared. He stood on the top of Trumpet Hill, between Carlingford and Dundalk, and threw boulders, rocks and stones at Queen Maeve's army.

Cuculan was an excellent shot. He killed so many of Queen Maeve's warriors she became very worried and thought, 'My army can't win the battle with Cuculan. I wonder if he'd agree to take part in single combat?'

Single combat means each side in a war picks a champion to fight for them and the war's won by the winner. It keeps a lot of people from being killed and is a very sensible idea. Cuculan agreed because it meant he could fight one warrior at a time and not the whole army.

Queen Maeve decided one of her warriors, called Loch, was to act as her champion.

He said he'd rather go home, but she said, 'Loch, get out there and kill Cuculan or I'll kill you!' So Loch decided he'd nothing to lose. If he fought Cuculan there was a slight chance he might survive, and if he didn't Queen Maeve would murder him.

Queen Maeve was a nasty woman! She guldered, 'I appoint my champion Loch to fight you at the Yellow Ford.'

Cuculan yelled, 'Right you are! I'm on my way.'

Queen Maeve.

The Morrigan thought, 'He won't fancy me in my ordinary shape. I'll change into a beautiful young woman, with long fair hair, flashing blue eyes and a gorgeous dress of many colours.'

She changed shape, walked up to Cuculan and smiled.

He scowled at her. He was cross. How dare she walk into a war zone? Was she not right in the head? She could get killed.

The Morrigan thought Cuculan's expression was cute so she said, 'Cuculan, I love you.' Remember she was the Goddess of War so she loved angry people.

He shouted, 'Clear off, you edjiot!'

The Morrigan smiled and said, 'I love you and you could at least be polite.'

'I said CLEAR OFF! You're two sandwiches short of a picnic!'

The Morrigan was annoyed. 'Watch it wee lad,' she snarled, 'or I'll bust you.'

'You and what army?'

'I don't need an army. I'll turn into an eel and trip you, I'll cause cattle to stampede and run you down. I'll become a she-wolf and eat you!'

Cuculan laughed, did a big loud smelly one and shouted, 'I'll smash your ribs with my toes, throw stones at you and burst your eyes, or maybe I'll just break your legs.'

'I'll use my power to heal myself.'

'You don't scare me, Sunshine! I'll put a curse on you. You won't heal unless I bless you and I'll never bless you!'

The Morrigan decided she didn't love Cuculan, she hated him and he was very rude. She spat at him!

Spit not only looks revolting, but it's full of germs.

She turned back into a raven, flew to the top of a tree, stood on a branch and shouted, 'Wow-ab-ab-ab-a-duk!' – which according to my grandson, Cadan, is the rudest thing an animal can say.

Queen Maeve's champion, Loch, met him and the fight began.

It was tough! Loch was a great warrior. His body was covered in snakeskin armour that made Cuculan's sword bounce off it.

They moved back and forward up and down the ford in deadly combat.

The Morrigan turned herself into a huge eel and wrapped three coils of her long body around Cuculan's legs. He stumbled and fell.

Loch saw his opportunity and slashed Cuculan with his sword. Blood gushed into the waters of the ford, turning it red.

Cuculan thrust his sword into the eel.

There was a puff of smelly smoke. The eel disappeared and a herd of cattle appeared.

The Morrigan turned into a she-wolf and snarled at them, so they stampeded.

Cuculan lifted a stone, took careful aim and burst one of her eyes.

The Morrigan yelled, 'Wow-ab-ab-ab-a-duk!', turned into a red heifer, went back to the herd of cows and stood in front of them.

They were very surprised to have a new leader, so they all did big smelly ones!

Cows' smelly ones are made of methane gas and each cow produces about 120kg of methane gas each year.

Do you weigh as much as 120kg? What weight are you?

Do you think you could ever become as heavy as the amount of methane gas a cow produces each year doing smelly ones?

Do you do smelly ones?

Every smelly one adds to the amount of methane gas in the atmosphere. So do those done by dogs, cats and other animals. There's an awful lot of methane gas in our atmosphere! In the past, Earth could deal with it, but it can't cope today because there are too many people and too many animals, and we are suffering from global warming because the gas acts like a thermal blanket keeping heat on the earth.

The Morrigan looked at the cows, turned towards Cuculan, guldered, 'Come on girls!' and charged. She hoped to trample Cuculan into the dirt.

Cuculan threw a rock that broke her legs before seeing a weak spot in Loch's armour. Shouting, 'Here! Take this!', he stuck his spear into Loch's stomach. Loch fell flat

Come on girls! Charge!

on his face in water and Cuculan cut his head off!

Cuculan had lost a lot of blood. He was exhausted. He went and hid among the trees and sat with his head in his hands.

The Morrigan dragged herself away from the ford, lay down and cried her eyes out.

'I was beautiful,' she sobbed, 'and look at me now! I've only got one eye. My chest's sore. I can just about drag myself along. Cuculan won't help. He won't bless me.

Come on Daisy! Let's trick him.

Maybe I could trick him … He's very polite … He's lost a lot of blood … He's bound to be thirsty … If I gave him a drink of milk he'd bless me!'

She turned into an old woman, hid her blind eye under straggly dirty hair and limped towards Cuculan, leading an old cow.

Cuculan said, 'I'm very thirsty. Could you give me a drink of milk? Please?'

The Morrigan milked the cow into an earthenware bowl. He drank it, felt better and said, 'Thank you kindly and bless you.'

'Ha! Ha! Ha!' laughed the Morrigan, 'I thought you said you'd never bless me!' She turned back into a raven and flew away to cause more trouble – but that's another story.

3

THE DRAGONS ON BELFAST'S CAVE HILL

My friend John Gray told me this story about forty years ago. Is that old enough to qualify? In all honesty I don't know. I like it so I'm going to tell it because it explains something I always wondered about.

I can't quite remember John's story exactly, so my version might be slightly different. That's what happens with folk tales. They change a bit over time, unless they are learnt off by heart.

Belfast is a beautiful city surrounded by hills. When I was wee you could stand in the middle of the city, look up and see them.

Unfortunately houses have been built on the Castlereagh Hills so you can't see green hills to the east of the city, but you can still see the Cave Hill. It towers above Belfast and has a huge cliff called Napoleon's Nose.

I grew up in Belfast and I often saw small fires on the Cave Hill and wondered what caused them. I asked my mummy and she said it was the farmers burning gorse.

I didn't think that was right so I asked Granda Finlay.

Granda said, 'I think those fires are caused by magic dragons we can't see. Let's go and have a look and see if we can find out. It's a long walk. Are you game? We could bring Scamp.'

I was game. I loved going for long walks with Granda. He was fun. He used to do interesting things like call the cows to the gates of fields and talk to them. He grew up in the country and knew how to call the cows and what they were saying and he told me.

Mummy said Granda was an 'auld fool' but if I wanted to go with him and look for dragons that was all right with her, so off we went.

It was a long walk, up through Belfast Castle grounds and on to the hills, along the steep path past the three caves.

Granda told me in the distant past many people were so poor they couldn't afford a house so they lived in caves.

He said, 'Naughty people lived in the big cave at the bottom of the cliff. They made it into a shebeen. That's a place where you can buy Mountain Dew, an illegal drink also called poiteen! It's the strongest alcoholic drink you can get. It would blow your head off!'

I agreed that was a bad thing, but we couldn't blame them. Granda said, 'When I was a lad you couldn't come into the castle grounds because the game warden would have shot you! Lots of people were starving so they went into big estates, like this, to hunt rabbits and deer.

'The people who owned the land lived in the big houses and had plenty to eat. They didn't like starving people stealing rabbits and deer so they put signs up saying, "Trespassers will be shot" and hired gamekeepers to shoot strangers. It didn't matter if the person shot was killed because he'd been warned!'

I was shocked!

It was very difficult to walk on the top of Cave Hill. One minute I had to take a big step up and the next step was away down a hole.

Granda said, 'The way the land goes up and down in ridges is what remains of the old lazy beds.'

I asked what lazy beds were. He said, 'In the late 1700s and early 1800s there were so many people living in Ireland every square inch of land was used to grow potatoes. People hadn't anything to eat, apart from potatoes, so they grew them everywhere, even on top of mountains. You can see the land up here's very wet. If you planted potatoes in it they would rot.

'Farmers were very crafty. They put a line of manure on top of the earth, placed their potatoes on top, dug a trench beside the line and put the earth from the trench on top of the potatoes.

'That was very clever because the trench drained water off the land and the farmers saved time because they didn't dig a whole field, only half of it. That's why they're called lazy beds.

'There was a great famine beginning in 1845. The potato crop failed for several years in a row and many people either died of hunger or emigrated. The population became so scarce it hasn't recovered. That's

I think those flames are caused by dragons.

why potatoes aren't grown up there and all we can see is the remains of the old lazy beds.'

When Granda and I were on top of the Cave Hill it was covered by wild heather and gorse. The gorse was on fire and we didn't see anybody!

We watched the fires for some time. The flames spread slowly but sometimes we could see a small ripple pass over them.

Granda said, 'I think invisible dragons might be eating the gorse.'

I agreed and didn't think much more about it until my friend, John Gray, told me the following story.

A long time ago in the 1930s a boy, called, Michael, who was 12 years of age, lived with his mummy and daddy in Clara Street, in east Belfast. He went to Elmgrove Primary School and was miserable because three nasty boys, Scrap, Mitcher and Mosey, bullied him, and his mummy was very house proud. She was so fussy she'd have made the sun wipe its feet before it came in the house! The sun never got in because the blinds were kept shut so it wouldn't fade the furniture.

Everybody told Michael he lived in a little palace. He thought he'd rather live in a house, so he could get covered in mud without being scolded and his mummy wasn't always polishing furniture or fluffing up cushions. He didn't have any brothers or sisters, so he was very lonely.

One day Scrap crept up behind him and hissed, 'I'm going to knock the melt out of you on the way home from school!'

Michael was so scared he did a soft smelly one and ran towards his house as fast as his legs would carry him out.

Scrap nearly caught him outside Boxy's shop, but Michael dashed inside and stood there panting.

Nobody knew why Boxy was called Boxy. Perhaps it was because he had so many boxes in his shop, or perhaps because he'd once been a boxer?

His mother said he was a 'scruffy old man' but Michael liked him. He was interesting, very wise and full of stories about the time he'd been a sailor and had travelled the world.

Boxy said, 'Hello Michael, is that big bully outside annoying you?'

Michael was so upset he couldn't answer. Boxy smiled and said, 'My old women has made some apple tart. I think she'd give you a share.'

He opened the door at the back of the shop and led Michael into his cosy kitchen.

'Wife,' he said, 'here's a young fella whose tongue is hanging out for a piece of tart.'

Boxy's wife drew a chair up in front of the American stove. (It looked something like the wood-burning stoves we have today but it burnt coal and had a lid on the top so you could drop fuel on the fire. It was used for cooking. There's one in one of the houses in the Ulster Folk and Transport Museum at Cultra. That's on the main road between Holywood and Bangor, County Down.)

The shop bell sounded. Boxy answered, served a customer, returned and sat down with a cup of tea in one hand and a piece of tart in the other. 'Michael,' he said, 'have you ever thought about getting a pet? I think a boy such as you could do with one.'

'I can't have a pet. I'd love a dog, but Mummy says dogs are smelly, they'd poo in the yard, cause a mess and drop hairs all over the place. She won't let me have a cat 'cos she says cats give her the shivers and they'd probably scratch our nice new settee and I can't have a rabbit, or a guinea pig, or a hamster, or even a fish.

'She says a pet would be a nuisance and she'd end up looking after it.'

Boxy said, 'You need something special, something magical, something like a dragon. Come to the back door and look at the Cave Hill.

'Do you see that big cliff beyond the ships and the cranes? Do you see the three caves where people used to live? They are deep and black as soot. Dragons live there now.

'Do you see patches of smoke drifting over the hill caused by young dragons eating gorse?

'Tell you what, Michael, next Saturday take a wee dander round Smithfield. Go to the pet shop in Gresham Street, walk past it and look carefully at all the doors. There's a magic shop run by an old man. He has baby dragons and he might give you one.

'If there's magic in the air you'll see a special door. I can't describe it but you'll recognise it. Go inside and see what happens.'

Michael was so excited he did big loud smelly ones, so he sounded like a motorbike all the way home!

That night he dreamt of dragons. At first he was frightened but the dragons were friendly. A baby one smiled and rubbed its scaly head against him. He woke up and thought, 'I'd love a pet dragon!'

Next Saturday, Michael got up early, walked down the Castlereagh Road, over the Albert Bridge and into the centre of Belfast. He went past the big Albert Clock, up High Street, along the side of the Bank Buildings (they burnt down last year but are being rebuilt) and into Gresham Street. He stood outside the pet shop and looked at the puppies in the window. There was a cute little black and white one with a curly tail and big eyes. It came over to the window, looked at Michael and seemed to say, 'I'd love to be your dog!'

Michael gulped and walked slowly up the street looking carefully at the doors. Suddenly he saw a strange shop. It didn't have a name, the paintwork was peeling and covered with peculiar signs. There was nothing in the window, just a black curtain. He turned the handle and went in.

An old man with a long black beard stood at the back of the shop. He said, 'Come this way Michael, I've been expecting you.' He opened the door to another room. It was very dark and everything had a weird glow.

The old man went over to a door in the back and opened a furnace that was burning fiercely inside. He took a shovel, and, quick as a flash, thrust it into the flames, pulled it out again, slammed the door shut and looked at what was on it. Nothing apart from ash and coals. He did the same thing again – nothing.

The old man sighed, 'Oh dear!' He said, 'It looks as if none of the baby dragons want to come and live with you. I can only try once more. Here goes, Fingers crossed!' He put the shovel back into the fire. When he

Look Michael! There's your dragon.

took it out again there was a tiny dragon that was glowing red hot. Its eyes sparkled like diamonds, wee puffs of smoke came out of its nose. It smiled up at Michael and wagged its tiny spiky tail.

'That's your dragon,' said the old man.

Michael nearly burst into tears, 'I haven't any money!' he gasped.

The old man laughed, 'You can't buy magic! You don't need money. Here you are, here's your dragon.'

Michael picked the dragon up and put it into his pocket. He was very happy. He walked home, opened the front door and went in. His mummy was sitting on the sofa having a wee cup of tea in her hand.

That's one of Ireland's strange sayings. 'Would you like a wee cup of tea in your hand?' doesn't mean anyone's going to pour tea into your hand. It means, 'Would you like a cup of tea (usually with a biscuit and a piece of cake) sitting beside the fire rather than at a table.'

Michael's mummy was tired so she was sitting on the sofa drinking tea and eating a bit of chocolate cake. She'd spent the whole day polishing, tidying, washing clothes, ironing, cooking and scrubbing floors and the outside step. When she was tired she was cross, so she snapped at Michael, 'Where have you been all day?'

'I walked down to Smithfield and an old man gave me a dragon.'

'Michael, how many times have I told you, you mustn't tell stories?'

'Honestly Mummy, I'm telling the truth. Look!' He lifted the dragon out of his pocket and held it out so his mummy could see it. She screamed!

A big flame shot out of the dragon's mouth and scorched one of her slippers.

Michael's dad came in through the front door.

'That looks interesting,' he said. 'What is it?'

The moment he spoke, the dragon stopped belching fire and flame, looked up, turned its head towards Michael's dad and smiled.

Michael's mother screamed, 'It's a wee monster! It's scorched one of my slippers.'

The dragon turned round, breathed another flame and scorched the other one.

Michael's dad laughed, 'Maisie,' he said, 'I think that dragon doesn't like hearing you scolding.'

The dragon immediately stopped belching flames and sat quietly in Michael's hand.

Michael's dad said, 'Michael I think you should put the dragon in the coal scuttle. It'll like being in there and it can see us while we have our tea.'

He opened out the gate-leg table, and Michael helped set it while his mother cooked a big fry of potato bread, soda bread, bacon, tomatoes, eggs and sausages.

Michael gave the dragon a piece of fried bread. The dragon spat it out.

Magic dragons know that fries aren't good for you. They're full of cholesterol that clogs up your arteries so your blood can't flow round your body properly, if you have them too often.

The dragon looked very happy in the coal scuttle. Michael's mum threw it a piece of coal. The dragon caught it in its mouth and everybody laughed.

Mum smiled and said, 'It's really cute, isn't it?'

Once the dishes were washed and dried they had a lovely night playing with the dragon.

At bedtime Mum said, 'The dragon can't go to bed with you, Michael. It might set the bedclothes on fire.'

Dad said, 'I think it'll be fine in the coal bucket. It looks happy and if it gets hungry it can always eat a piece of coal.'

Mum said, 'I think we should put it out in the yard to do a poo.'

Dad said, 'It's magic, so it doesn't poo, or do smelly ones. The only trouble is it won't stay long. Magic doesn't hang around.'

The family had a lovely weekend, the nicest Michael could remember. They went as usual to McQuiston Memorial Church in the morning, had Sunday lunch then walked up the Castlereagh Hills. It was a beautiful day and the dragon enjoyed looking at the marvellous view over Belfast.

Dad pointed out Harland and Wolff Shipyard, where the *Titanic* had been built.

Michael tried to look interested. Dad told him that every time they walked up there. Grown-ups are like that aren't they? They keep repeating themselves.

On Monday, Michael discovered the dragon had grown but it was still small enough to fit into his schoolbag so he took it to school. He popped some pieces of coal into his pockets so the dragon could have lunch. He'd a great time in the playground showing the dragon to his friends and explaining how he couldn't keep it for long. Scrap, Mitcher and Mosey looked as if they'd like to bully him but didn't dare come near because he had so many friends round him.

After school Scrap, Mitcher and Mosey chased Michael along the Beersbridge Road and caught up with him at the end of Clara Street. Mitcher grabbed him by the shoulders, while Scrap and Mosey yelled, 'What have you got in your schoolbag?'

Michael was very worried in case they hurt his precious dragon so he held it tight, kicked Mitcher's shins and yelled, 'Wind yer neck in.'

The dragon burst out of Michael's schoolbag. It was furious so it belched flames. Mosey did a big smelly one. Smelly ones are made of methane gas. It's easily set alight so Mosey's

Ha! Ha! Ha! Let that larn ye!

trousers went on fire. Michael laughed and laughed. The dragon set Scrap's and Mitcher's trousers on fire so they had to go home with bare bums! Their mums were very cross. They didn't believe their sons' trousers had been burnt by a dragon. They thought the boys had set their pants on fire by smoking.

That night the dragon flew away. Michael missed it but life had changed for him. Mum stopped spending all day every day polishing and cleaning. He was allowed to bring friends home and his house became a fun place to live.

Scrap, Mitcher and Mosey didn't bully him any more. They were scared because they thought Michael might have another dragon in his schoolbag!

Bullies are like that. They are cowards and if you stand up to them they run away. Best

I hope Michael knows I'm here.

of all, Dad came home with a puppy and Michael had a pet to love.

Michael never forgot his dragon. Sometimes, in bed at night, he heard drumming on the roof and knew his dragon was sitting there, and when he saw fires burning on Cave Hill he thought, 'My dragon and his friends are enjoying the fresh air and eating gorse. I bet that's more tasty than lumps of coal.'

4

CULAN'S HORRENDOUS HOUND

Hound awoke, stretched and growled. He was cross. He was always cross. He went over to the edge of his cage and looked out through the bars. The warriors and their wives were preparing for the night. The huge gates in the fence were shut and vats of mead were being carried into the house.

Hound howled, 'WOOOOOOOOOO-HHHHHHHHH! WOOOOOOOOOH! WOOOOOOOOH!'

The sound sent shivers up the spines of all those who heard it, except Culan, who thought, 'That hound is a fantastic watchdog! It'll eat intruders on sight.

'Now, is everyone safely inside? Hound'll kill you if he sees you.'

Culan did a head count of his wife and children, King Conor and his courtiers. They were all there.

'Right you are,' he said, 'I'll feed Hound and let him out.'

Culan was very pleased with himself. He was very rich, the best blacksmith in the land.

He made shields, spears, swords and needles by royal appointment for King Conor himself.

He'd invited King Conor and his courtiers to spend the night. The party was going well. The king drank a lot of mead, enjoyed stories told by the bard, laughed at the juggler and enjoyed the dancing girls!

Culan smiled. 'King Conor's bound to give me a big order. He's got a nephew, Setanta. The wee nipper shows great promise as a warrior. He's bound to need to be kitted out.'

Then he thought, 'I can make needles! I wonder if I could sell a few needles to the ladies in King Conor's court?'

Think about needles. They are very small and they must have a sharp point and an eye that thread can be passed through.

That's a very difficult thing to make from red-hot iron and the type of instruments used to make horse shoes! Very few blacksmiths have the necessary skill.

Hound wagged his tail and barked when he saw Culan, who was carrying six dead hens and a dead pig. He opened the gate

I'd eat ye as soon as look at ye!

of the pen, petted Hound, and said, 'Here boy! Grub's up! I've important guests staying tonight. Take good care of us.'

Hound barked, wagged his tail and thought, 'If anybody dares put their neb out of yon door I'll chew their legs off.'

Cuculan went back to his guests and said, 'Last week a scoundrel climbed over the fence. It was a wild night, the rain was pelting down and the wind was howling. During the night Hound woke me. He was barking and howling. I heard someone scream and thought, "A burglar must have climbed the fence. I should go and see what's happening." It was a wild night so I thought, "I'll find out in the morning." I snuggled up under my nice warm wolfskins and went back to sleep.

'Next day I wondered if I'd been dreaming. I went to lock Hound up. I keep him in his kennel during the day because he'd kill anyone he saw. He's my dog. He loves me but anyone else is dead meat.'

'I walked around outside and couldn't see anything. I thought, "All's in order! I must have been dreaming," then I found it. It was lying against the fence, a leather boot with a bit of chewed leg sticking out of it!

'I looked more carefully and found traces of blood here, there and everywhere.

'A burglar must have climbed the fence and Hound ate him. The only thing left was one boot and a whole lot of blood stains. Good for Hound!'

Culan was in the middle of making a speech welcoming King Conor when there was a terrible commotion outside: screams, yells and frantic barking followed by a terrible gurgling sound.

King Conor went white, 'I forgot about Setanta,' he groaned. 'I asked him if he'd like to come with me. He was playing hurling with the Boys Brigade. He said he wanted to finish the game and he'd catch up with me.'

Culan gasped, 'If he's managed to get into the stockade, Hound'll eat him.' He nearly wet himself. He knew King Conor loved his nephew. He'd hoped the king would buy a complete set of armour for his nephew. He couldn't do that if Setanta was dead and, worse than that, he'd lose his royal customer! He couldn't care less about Setanta. The only thing he cared about was money. He opened the door and looked out.

King Conor stood behind him with his heart in his mouth. He loved Setanta and didn't want him to be eaten by Hound. The other guests stood behind the two men and peered through the gloom and SCREAMED! One of the dancing girls fainted and a warrior did an unexpected poo! There are times when wee smelly ones are not to be trusted!

A large white shape was rising in the air and beating itself against the ground.

Boom … Boom … BOOM.

One of the courtiers yelled, 'Inside everyone! It's a ghost! It's out to get us.'

King Conor peered out into the night. He didn't believe in ghosts and he wanted to find Setanta so he yelled, 'Setanta. Setanta! SETANTA! where are you?'

A cheery voice shouted, 'Here, Uncle King Conor!' The white shape stopped hitting the ground and Setanta ran towards the door dragging Hound along behind him.

Culan gasped in horror, 'He's killed Hound! The wee …' He stopped himself saying a string of bad words as he remembered who Setanta was.

Setanta reached the door, stood smiling and said, 'Culan, I'm sorry about your dog. When I arrived the gate was shut so I did my salmon leap over the fence and was walking towards the door when I heard snarling and barking behind me. I looked back and saw Hound. He was mad, slabbering at the mouth with his red eyes glowing like coals. He was going to eat me.

'I thought the best thing I could do was knock him out so I put my hurling ball on the ground and used my stick to aim it at Hound's forehead. Hound moved his head so the ball stuck in his throat. The poor dog was in agony so I put him out of his misery by banging his head against the ground.'

Culan's face went bright purple with the effort of stopping himself giving Setanta a

Good dog! Did yer man taste nice?

good kicking. (He was a Celt and grown up Celts frequently hit or kicked children.) He stuttered, 'Immmm'd glaaaaad you're not hurt, buuuut how do I protect myyyyyy property? Hoooooound was priceless. Now he's dead I'll be robbed. I don't know what to do.'

Setanta smiled as he said, 'Dinnae worry! Hound died in battle. His soul'll go straight to the Afterworld. He sired some great pups, didn't he? Train one of them up to be a guard dog and I'll look after your property 'til it's ready.'

Culan looked doubtful, turned to King Conor and asked, 'What do you think of that?'

'I think it's a great idea. Setanta killed Hound so he's shown himself capable of dealing with any danger that comes his way.'

Setanta was as good as his word. He looked after Culan's property until another dog was reared. From that day until the day he died, Setanta was nicknamed Cuculan. In Irish 'Cu' means hound, and Culan was Hound's owner so Setanta's new name, Cuculan, means 'Culan's hound'.

Setanta also became known as The Hound of Ulster because he was a champion warrior who guarded Ulster. He lived in Dundalk in a place called Dun Dealgan. Names change through time so Dun Dealgan changed to Dundalk.

You can visit the place where Cuculan lived. It's a good place for a picnic, if you don't mind a walk up a steep hill. There's a great view from the top. It's not well sign-posted. Go to Dundalk and find the Armagh Road. Dun Dealgan is marked by a confusing sign that says 'Castletown'! An Elizabethan tower house was built on the site in the sixteenth century. That's a long time after Cuculan died, so now his old home is called Castletown. People in Dundalk are very friendly so if you get lost ask somebody for directions.

5

KING
OF
THE
BIRDS

Once upon a time in days of old, when men were bold and monkeys chewed tobacco, the birds of the air had an argument in the forest that once covered Ireland. Eagle had called a meeting to decide who'd be crowned King of the Birds. He stood high on the topmost branch of a tree and shouted, 'Humans have kings so we should choose one, too. I'm big and strong. I should be king.'

Crow disagreed: 'I should be crowned because I have such a beautiful voice.'

'Huh!' sneered Sparrow, 'Humans tell bad singers, "You've a voice like a crow!"'

'Beautiful voice, my bum! I'm the bird with a beautiful voice,' snarled Nightingale.

The other birds thought that was stupid and said, 'Kings don't have to sing!'

'Aaahoo, awooo, to wit to woo,' said the owl, 'Kings should be clever. Have you ever heard the old saying, "As wise as an owl?" I'm wise, so I should be king.'

'Don't make me laugh!' sneered the seagull, 'You're a dimwit!'

When wren said he should be king of the birds, Eagle laughed.

'Sure you're no bigger than a sparrow's fart.'

Sure you're no bigger than a sparrow's fart!

Wren was very annoyed, so did what he always did when he was annoyed. He very, very quietly, so nobody could hear him, said nursery rhymes his old granny had taught him:

Dan, Dan was a funny wee man,
He washed his face in a frying pan,
He combed his hair with a donkey's tail,
And scratched his belly
With his big toe nail!

Humpty Dumpty sat on a wall,
Humpty Dumpty had a great fall.
All the king's horses and all the king's men
Said, 'Not scrambled eggs for breakfast again.'

That cheered him up so he remembered another one and muttered:

Mary had a little lamb,
She also had a bear,
I've often seen her little lamb
But I've never seen her bare!

He had a quiet little giggle, then listened carefully. It sounded as if the birds were beginning to agree.

Goose said, 'The bird who can fly the furthest should be king.'

Robin said, 'That's not fair because you fly thousands of miles each year while I have to stay at home guarding my territory.'

Eagle saw his opportunity and said, 'Birds are meant to fly, so our king should be a champion flyer. I agree flying long distances gives some birds an unfair advantage. Why don't we see who can get up the highest?'

Wren said, 'I agree!'

The other birds were astonished, 'You agree?'

'Yes! I agree. And a king should be brainy.'

'We all agree!' shouted the other birds.

They lined up and flew way, way up into the sky. That is all except Wren. He was small and light so he climbed on top of Eagle's back and hid among his feathers.

As the birds flew higher and higher, they began to get tired and dropped out one by one.

Eagle flew on and on, up and up, until there were only a few left.

Wren looked down, felt dizzy and remembered his old granny saying, 'There's no gain without pain!' Then he thought, 'If I'm going to be King of the Birds I'll have to be brave. I must hang on like grim death and distract my mind so I don't die of fright!' So he forgot to be quiet and began singing one of old Granny's songs. It's a very good song to sing if you want to annoy somebody because you can keep repeating it:

Old King Cole was a merry old soul,
And a merry old soul was he.
He sent for a light
In the middle of the night to go to the W.C.
The moon shone bright on the closet wall,
The candle flame burned true,
But old King Cole fell down the hole
And got all covered in poo!
Old King Cole …

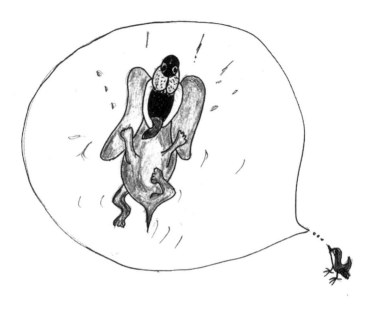

And the little dog laughed to see such fun,
so the cat did a little bit more.

Eagle heard the singing and looked around.
Stork was still flying upwards, as were
Albatross and Goose. He couldn't see anyone
else and thought, 'I must be imagining
things,' and gave himself a good shake. Wren
hung on like mad. He was lucky he didn't
fall off Eagle's back! He stopped singing and
whispered another nursery rhyme:

Hey diddle diddle,
The cat did a piddle
All over the kitchen floor.
The little dog laughed to see such fun,
So the cat did a little bit more.

Eagle became exhausted. He couldn't go any higher. Wren smiled to himself.

Eagle laughed, 'That's done it! All the other birds have dropped back so I'm King of the Birds.'

Wren flew off Eagle's back and shouted, 'No you're not!' and flew above Eagle. 'I'm higher than you. I'm King of the Birds.'

Eagle was furious! He tried to fly higher but couldn't. He was too tired. 'You cheat!' he yelled. 'I flew higher than you! You just sat on my back!'

'But we agreed whoever got up highest should be king. I used my brains to get above you and kings should have good brains. I outwitted you so I'm King of the Birds.'

The other birds agreed and Wren was crowned King of the Birds.

6

SAINT
PATRICK
AND
THE
SNAKES

(Reproduced with the kind permission of the executors of Crawford Howard)

Crawford Howard was a very dear old friend. I was upset when he died some years ago. He was great fun and I loved storytelling with him.

Crawford said his verse was 'rubbish'! I have to agree with him, but that doesn't matter. It's funny, isn't it? For several years he taught English as a foreign language in Spain. You'd never guess that from the ungrammatical fun things he wrote! He used words that used to be common but are disappearing. This is what they mean: lep means big jump, outta means out of, herpled means walk as fast as possible with a limp and possibly using a stick, bake and gub mean the same thing – face. They can also mean mouth. Dozer means very slow and sleepy.

Ireland has a tradition of writing comic verse and Crawford's part of it. He used to make me laugh so hard I nearly wet my knickers! Why don't you see if you can make people laugh by writing some comic verse?

There never were any snakes in Ireland, so St Patrick couldn't banish them. You can't banish what you haven't got! Millions of years ago Ireland and England were joined on to the rest of Europe. Ireland broke away and became a separate island and the snakes couldn't cross the Irish Sea. They did manage to reach England before it became separated from Europe but not Ireland, so Crawford's 'poem' is a load of nonsense!

St Patrick and the Snakes

You've heard of the snakes in Australia,
You've heard of the snakes in Japan,
You've heard of the rattler – that old
    Texas battler,
Whose bite can mean death to a man.
They've even got snakes in auld England,
    Nasty adders all yellow and black,

But in Erin's fair Isle, we can say with a smile,
They're away and they're not coming back.

Now years ago things was quite different,
There were servants all over the place.
If ye climbed up a ladder ye might meet
    an adder,
Or a cobra might lep at yer face.
If ye went for a walk up the Shankill,
Or a dander along Sandy Row,
A flamin' great python would likely come
    writhin'
An' take a great lump outta yer toe.

There once was a guy called St Patrick,
A preacher of fame and renown
An' he hoisted his sails and came over
    from Wales,
To convert all the heathen in Down.
An' he herpled about through the country
With a stick and a big pointy hat,
An' he kept a few sheep that he sold on the
    cheap,
But sure there's no money in that.

He was preachin' a sermon in Comber
And getting quite carried away
When he mentioned that Rome had once
    been his home
And that was the wrong thing to say,
For he felt a sharp bite on his cheekbone
An stuck a han' up til his bake
An the thing that had lit on his gub and
    had bit,
Was a wee Presbyterian snake.

Now the snake slithered down from the pulpit,
Expecting St Patrick to die,
But yer man was no dozer – he lifted his
    crozier,
An' belted the snake in the eye.
Says he to the snake, 'Listen legless
Ye'd better take yerself off
If ye think that that trick will work on
    St Patrick,
Ye must be far worser than daft!'

So the snake slithered home in a temper,
An gathered his friends all around,

Says he, 'Listen mates, we'll get on our
    skates,
I reckon it's time to leave town.
It's no fun when ye bite a big fella,
An' sit back and expect him to die,
And he's so flamin' quick with yon big
    crooked stick
That he hits ye a dig in the eye.'

So a strange sight confronted St Patrick
When he woke the very next day.
The snakes, with long faces were all packing
    their cases,
And heading for Donegal Quay.
Some got on cheap flights to Majorca
And some booked apartments in Spain.
They were all headin' out and there wasn't
    a doubt
They weren't comin' back again.

So the reason the snakes left auld Ireland,
(An' this is no word of a lie)
They all went to place to bite people's faces
And be reasonably sure that they'd die.

The snake slithered home in a temper.

An' the auld snakes still caution their
  grandsons,
For God's sake beware of St Pat
An take yourselves off if you see his big
  staff,
An' his coat an' his big pointy hat

Crawford Howard

7

THE
FATE
OF
FINN
McCOOL'S
FAVOURITE
DOGS

Most giants are scary. They're hungry, eat children, put spells on beautiful princesses, lock them up in towers and shout nasty things like, 'Fee, Fi Fo Fum, I smell a dirty bum!'

Most giants hate everybody except their mothers, who are disgusting old hags with runny noses and dribble running down their chins! You don't want to be near a giant's mother because she keeps doing big smelly ones!

Finn McCool was different. He was gentle. He loved his sister, Fiona, and doted on her children, Bran and Skeolan. He hunted, fought battles and did great deeds with the Fianna. He was normally good tempered but he lost his temper with the Scottish giant Bennadonner and built the Giant's Causeway so he could cross the sea and knock the melt out of him, and he was furious when a wicked wizard set Tara on fire every year for twenty-three years.

Tara was the home of the High Kings of Ireland – in other words, it was very important. It was founded by a queen called Tea! When she died her grave was called Tea-Mur or the House of Tara. Over time Tea-main changed into Temair and eventually into Tara.

Thousands of years ago Tara was a city. It's in County Meath. The original city has disappeared but you can still see the remains of earthen ditches and banks that once protected it. There's a beautiful view from the highest point and I enjoyed running up and down the banks, although I had to be careful not to fall and break my neck!

Feasts used to be held in Tara's banqueting hall. The kings and queens invited everyone from the whole of Ireland. Imagine that! You could be a tramp and you get an invitation from the king to come to a feast in a hall that seated 1,000 diners at a time!

Finn McCool was furious when he heard the wizard went every year to feasts at Tara and played magic music to make everyone go to sleep. When everyone was soundly snoring the wizard set the place on fire.

Finn McCool decided he was going to go to a feast and to stay awake. Whenever the wizard played his harp Finn stuck the point of his sword into the palm of his hand. It hurt so he couldn't sleep!

When the wizard saw everyone was asleep he laughed, belched, did a big loud smelly one, stopped playing his harp and began setting the place on fire. Finn McCool jumped up and killed him.

The other wizards were annoyed with Finn McCool because he'd killed one of their friends. They didn't dare attack him, so got their revenge by turning Fiona's children into dogs.

One day when Finn McCool was hunting with Bran and Skeolan they smelt a witch on the slopes of Slieve Bloom. They hated wizards and witches, so decided to kill her and ran after her.

The witch was very frightened. She knew the dogs could run like lightning so she turned herself into a deer. The witch ran for her life as Bran and Skeolan chased her the length and breadth of Ireland. Eventually she became tired and the dogs began to catch

Do you smell a witch?

up with her in County Donegal. She was terrified and gasping for breath, so she spun round and cast a spell that turned them into rock. They were going so fast they couldn't stop until they'd travelled forty miles. They came to a halt in County Fermanagh and turned into two small mountains, Big Dog and Little Dog. If you go to Fermanagh's Big Dog Forest you can climb them.

8

MOYRY CASTLE'S KILLER CAT

There's a steep road leading from the North of Ireland through the Slieves of County Armagh and the Mountains of Louth into the South. It's called 'The Gap of the North' and it has a strange haunted atmosphere. It's a place where the birds never sing as a mark of respect for all those who died there in battle. It's filled with ghosts and feels as if it's full of danger, a real Bearna Baoghall (Gap of Danger).

It was here Queen Elizabeth's soldiers built Moyry Castle in 1601. It's what's known as an 'Elizabethan Tower House' and you can visit the ruins. It was originally a tall square building that once controlled the border between County Armagh and County Louth. A warden and a garrison of men lived in it.

Moyry Castle was a strange building because it didn't have any stairs. Ladders were used to get from one floor to another.

It had a lot of places for guns. The drawbridge leading to the entrance had a hole above the door used to pour boiling oil and other nasty things, like buckets of piddle and poo, on top of unwanted visitors.

One day a strange old man with a large tiger cat came out of the woods and walked up to the drawbridge. He told the warden he was a wizard who'd visited all the castles in the country. He asked if he could come in and entertain the troops.

The guards invited him in and enjoyed watching him juggling and doing magic tricks. His tiger cat was fantastic! It jumped through rings of fire!

The wizard told the soldiers his tiger had been abandoned by its mother and he'd hand-reared it. He said, 'I love that big cat as if it was my own child and it loves me. It's very affectionate. It follows me around like a dog. It protects me and keeps anyone from hurting me. He can be the wild fierce boy and kill people but he likes my friends and doesn't attack them.'

Every time the cat did a trick the wizard gave it a treat and it rolled over and purred.

The guards enjoyed the performance and

paid for it, so the wizard said he'd call again sometime in the future.

The wizard and the huge cat went and lived in a cave in the mountains. Each day the cat foraged for food. When the wizard gave a shrill whistle it replied with a loud 'murrow' and came bounding back with prey in its mouth.

The wizard stroked and petted the cat and gave it catnip treats before cooking the prey over an open fire, dividing it into two and giving half to the cat.

The big cat didn't kill for pleasure. It just killed enough to feed them, and at night they slept curled up together, covered by furs on a soft pile of leaves, as snug as bugs in a rug.

Eventually the wizard and the cat set out on their travels again. They were away for a long time and the guards at Moyry Castle had changed by the time they came back. The new soldiers weren't friendly. When the wizard went up to the drawbridge a sentry shot him dead with his bow and arrow.

The cat was furious. He took a deep breath and jumped up on the ramparts.

GRRRRRRRRRRRRRR!

The sentry didn't see the cat, but a shadow made him wonder what was going on.

'Who goes there?' he shouted.

'Mur-row!' mewed the cat.

"Ha! Ha! Ha!' laughed the sentry, 'You Irish have very peculiar names. Well Mur-row, where do you come from?'

'Maaa-yo.'

All cats come from Mayo.

'What's the password?' yelled the sentry.

'Three blind mice,' replied the cat.

'Rats!' shouted the sentry.

The cat saw red at the sentry's rudeness. He pounced and sank his teeth into his skull. It shattered with a terrible crunching sound. The noise woke a second sentry who was dozing on the other side of the keep, and he came to see what was happening. The cat tore his throat out!

The sight of so much blood made the cat go mad with a blood lust. He went silently from room to room killing all the garrison's soldiers by cracking their skulls open and shredding their flesh into mincemeat.

When he'd avenged his master's death he washed the blood off his fur, curled up into a ball and fell asleep.

He was wild with grief and rage and started killing all the animals he met, dragging their bodies back to Moyry Castle and eating them. He thought all humans were evil, except his master. He pounced on travellers and shattered their skulls and tore their throats, and he spent a lot of time sitting on the castle ramparts howling horribly.

One day the big cat caught a toddler in his jaws, carried it off to a clearing in the woods, set it on the ground and played cat and mouse. He allowed it to crawl away then pounced and carried it back to the centre of the clearing in his ferocious jaws. The poor baby was terrified and screamed. Luckily a group of O'Hanlon's men heard him, saw what was happening and rushed at the cat with their long spears. The cat realised it was outnumbered, backed into a thicket and snarled before disappearing into the woods.

The toddler wasn't hurt. He was taken back to his mother, who was crying her eyes out because she thought her son was dead.

The big cat terrorised the countryside. It was clever and cunning. Once, when surrounded by local men it sprang up a tree and had fun by putting its nose round the trunk and making cat laugh sounds as arrows pinged into the bark. Eventually it sprang over their heads and vanished.

Traps and snares were set but the cat had a sixth sense warning it of danger and he was able to avoid them.

People became scared to go out alone.

Gradually the pain of his master's death faded and the cat began to enjoy living on his own. He could come and go as he pleased and life was easier because he'd only one mouth to feed. He began to think of himself as King of the Castle. He realised he was free. Then he thought, 'All cats should be free. Humans shouldn't keep cats as slaves. It's against their cat rights!' He decided to start a cat league for the emancipation of cats. He became ambitious and wanted to be recognised as King of the Cats, a Catamount.

One night, when he felt the time was ripe for a revolution, he stood erect on Moyry Castle's battlements and gave a loud cat-call summoning all the cats in the neighbour-hood to hear what he had to say. He stood proudly on his hind legs with his front paws supported on a battlement and addressed the crowd. He realised a lot of big words begin with the word 'cat' so he used as many 'cat' words as possible. There's a copy of his speech below. I admit, I don't know what all the 'cat' words mean. Do you? Can you find out?

Friends, I say by Bubastis the wife of Pthah and the goddess of cats, humans keep us as slaves to kill rats and mice. Slavery is wrong. It should cease. Cats should be free.

We must stop killing rats and mice. What harm has a rat or a mouse done to a cat? We should kill humans instead.

Each cat must sign its name in a catalogue as a Member of The League for the Extermination of the Human Race and the Emancipation of Cats.

We will stop being catspaws. We must realise we are the cats' pyjamas. We must cause a catastrophe that wipes the human race off the face of the earth. We must put all humans in the same category. They are slave owners. They must die!

We must cause a catastrophe.

Now listen carefully while I catechise you how to act.

Catenate yourselves in a great chain, surround the houses and catacaluptify all the inhabitants. When they are seized with catalepsy lay them out on catafalques and bury them in catacombs.

Tomorrow we will meet carrying catapults. Only those with cataracts are excused.

Any cat that fails to come up to scratch shall be cursed and lose its nine lives.

Beware of the cataclysm engineered by me, your Catamount.

When we have won the battle I, your leading cat, your Catamount, your King of the Cats, shall stand erect to receive you.

There was great clapping of paws, and the cats swore they'd never lick fur again until they'd licked their enemies.

The Catamount gave them the secret sign and disappeared into the night.

Tom kitten didn't agree with the Catamount's plans. He loved his owners and told them about the plot.

When the people heard they were going to be attacked they had a meeting and decided the Catamount had to be killed.

Telltale cat.

Chief O'Hanlon said, 'We could send an armed posse but the cat would hear it coming and be warned. I think it would be better if one well-armed person sneaked up, caught the brute off guard and killed it.

Nobody wanted to face the cat alone so Chief O'Hanlon said he'd go. If he didn't come back in a reasonable time an armed posse should be sent out.

He dressed in his strongest armour, fetched his sword and shield and set off. He was careful not to make a sound. When he reached the castle he had a stroke of luck. The killer cat had eaten a lamb and was fast asleep curled up into a ball. Chief O'Hanlon crept up and sliced its head off.

I think it's a pity that Moyry Castle's guard murdered the wizard. If they hadn't done that there wouldn't have been a catalogue of disasters.

9

WHY SPIDERS ARE LUCKY

One cold December day I was sitting beside a cosy fire in an old cottage in the Ulster Folk and Transport Museum with my friend Linda Ballard, and she told me this story about a spider.

I like spiders. They have a bad reputation because some other countries have a few dangerous ones, like the black widow that is found in Australia. It has a poisonous bite and a nasty of habit of lurking under toilet seats and biting people's bare bums when they sit down!

Spiders are very useful animals. You should love them because they eat insects. If we didn't have spiders we'd die of starvation because there would be so many insects they'd destroy our food.

If you look at a spider's web you'll probably find it has caught flies, killed them and wrapped them up in strands of web to form a larder.

In the past, cobblers used sharp tools to mend footwear. If they cut themselves they stopped bleeding by wrapping cuts in spiders' webs. That sounds crazy unless you know webs

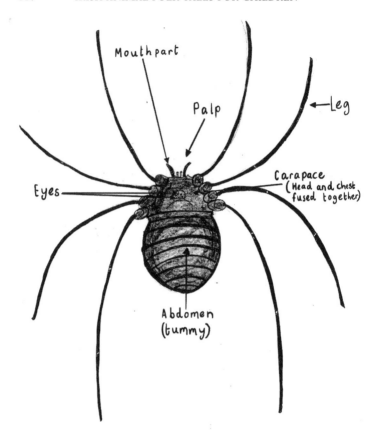

Spiders like me bring good luck.

are sterile and make good bandages. They are very fine so they catch blood cells coming out of a cut. That helps to form clots and stop the bleeding.

I admit spiders look sort of creepy with their eight legs and their feelers out on stalks, but I still like them. They can't help how they look and I'm sure they think we look peculiar with our two eyes and our ears on the side of our heads.

Our bodies are divided into three parts, head, chest and tummy, or if you want to use posh language, head, thorax and abdomen.

Our bodies have our heads at the top with our arms stuck on to our chests (thorax) while our legs hang out of the end of our tummies (abdomen).

Spiders' bodies have only two parts to their bodies. Their heads and chests are fused together to form a carapace and their tummies are joined on at the end.

Most spiders have six or eight eyes at the front of their carapace and they hear through hairs on their legs! They have feelers, called palps, at the front of their carapaces to feel things. The palps are very peculiar because when they feel something they can tell how it would taste! Wouldn't that be useful? I'd like to be able to know how something tastes without putting it into my mouth, wouldn't you?

Spider's mouths are very strange. They look like two thorns at the front of the carapace. They can't bite us but they can bite their prey, inject poison and eat their food by sticking their mouthparts into, say, a fly. The fatal injection they give turns the inside of the victim's body into a liquid so the spider can suck it up and only a dried-up skin is left.

I find spiders so interesting I've drawn one. Can you see all the bits I've described? Now I think I should get back to the story!

A long, long time ago an innkeeper's wife saw a spider sitting in the corner minding its own business. She didn't like it and nearly wet herself before lifting a brush and yelling, 'Get out you dirty brute! You're very ugly!' as she swept it out the door.

The poor spider was very upset. All of a sudden he was homeless and he'd been told he was dirty and ugly. He longed to find somewhere he could feel safe and hide. He crawled into the grass and looked around. There was no place to hang a web. He gave a big sigh because he loved spinning webs.

A jumping spider landed beside him and frightened him, so he ran as fast as his long legs would carry him and climbed a tree.

He had a lovely view and was happy until a bird tried to eat him. He quickly spun a long thread of web and swung, like Tarzan, on to the ground. He ran and ran and ran. Eventually he came to a cave and ran inside.

It was so dark he couldn't see anything.

'This is great,' he thought, 'I should be safe here and nobody'll see how ugly I am.'

He climbed up the wall, held on to the ceiling and looked carefully at it as he decided where he should hang his web. Suddenly he heard a noise and looked down. He was so surprised he'd have done a big loud smelly one, but he was a spider and spiders can't do that! His eyes had adapted to the light and he saw the cave was full of animals.

'Excuse me,' he said, 'I didn't mean to intrude. I didn't realise there was anyone here. I'll go away immediately.'

'Why go away?' said the cow, 'It's safe and dry here.'

'Bbbbbbbut bbbbbut I'm so ugly,' stammered the spider.

'I don't think you're ugly. Beauty's in the eye of the beholder. You're not ugly, you're just different! Now look at us. We are all different. Being different makes life interesting. You're very welcome.'

'That's right,' said the donkey, 'You're very welcome. In fact you're more than welcome because you'll be useful catching flies. They come in here and bite us.'

'Please stay,' said the sheep.

'You mean it? You really mean it? I can stay? I'm welcome?'

'YES!' shouted all the animals in a loud chorus.

The spider smiled as well as he could. (It's very hard to smile when you've a mouth that looks like two thorns, but he did his best.)

The spider was very happy living in the cave. He thought, 'I may be ugly but I can do good work. I'll spin the most beautiful web in the whole wide world.' He spun a web that was wide and thick. He made it rectangular in shape so it was different from all other spiders' webs. He was very proud of it and spent a lot of time sitting beside it and admiring it. When the weather turned cold he crept inside, curled up and was nice and warm.

One cold winter's night he was sleeping when he heard people talking. He looked down and saw a baby sleeping in the animals' manger. A young woman was gently touching the back of its neck. She turned round to the man and said, 'The baby's cold. I don't know what to do. I've put everything we have on him.'

The spider thought, 'My web would keep the baby warm.' Then he thought, 'My web's the most beautiful in the whole wide world. I can't bear to part with it. I'd be cold without it.'

Then he thought, 'I shouldn't be greedy. That poor baby's cold! Cold won't hurt me and I can spin another web. It'll take a long time but sure that doesn't matter.'

He cut the corners of his beautiful web and set it free. It drifted down and landed on the baby. The woman tucked it in, looked up and said, 'Thank you. That was a beautiful thing you did. Would you like to come down and see the baby?'

The spider was delighted. He jumped down and stood on the edge of the baby's bed. The baby was so beautiful that the spider smiled.

The lady said, 'Can I grant you a wish?'

The spider felt very excited, 'Yes! Please! Please make me beautiful.' He gasped, 'Please! Please! Please make me beautiful like a butterfly.'

The lady smiled as she said, 'I'm afraid I can't do that because beauty is in the eye of the beholder. What I can do is make you lucky.'

From that day to this, spiders have been lucky – so the next time you see one don't hurt it because it's a useful animal and it could bring you good luck.

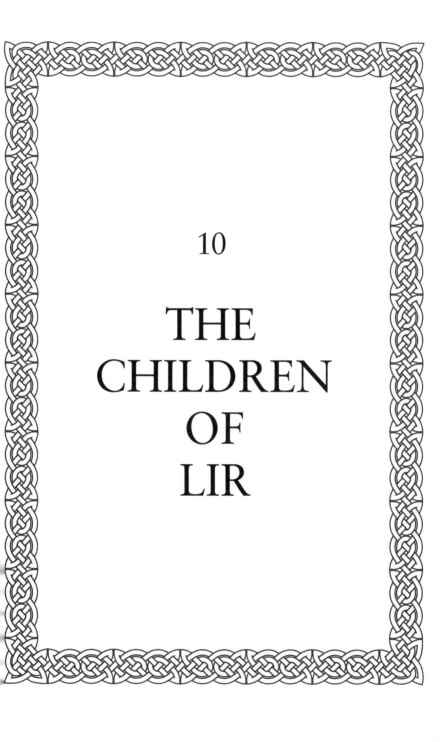

10

THE
CHILDREN
OF
LIR

The oral tradition says St Patrick loved a bit of craic and was never happier than when sitting round a fire listening to stories. He doesn't seem to have been a stuffy saint, all good deeds and no fun, and he had a bit of a temper, but that's another story. The oral tradition says this was his favourite story because it acts as a link between the old pagan beliefs and the new Christian religion.

A long time ago Ireland was inhabited by strange people called the Tuthna De Danaan, who were beautiful, very tall and never died. If they became very ill they fell into a deep sleep that lasted a thousand years.

Having people lying sleeping all round the place would have been an untidy nuisance, so the sleeping people were taken to a huge room under the sea and laid gently on beautiful beds until they woke up again.

The room under the sea was a nice place to wake up. It had floor-to-ceiling windows looking out on the sea. That meant you could waken up gradually and lie watching fish swim by until you felt like getting up. (That must have been lovely. I used to hate wakening up because my mum used to shout, 'Shift your lazy bum!' as she turned the lights on and pulled the bedclothes off me. It was very annoying!)

King Lir was King of the Tuthna De Danaan. He had a lovely wife called Eva, and two children, a girl called Fionuala and a boy called Aed. They were happy, or rather they would have been except Eva kept girning that she wanted another baby. Eventually she got her wish and had twin boys, Fiacre and Conn.

Unfortunately the effort of having two babies at once made her very, very tired, so she went into a deep sleep.

King Lir was terribly upset. He did a whole lot of big smelly ones, cried his eyes out, lifted Eva up in his arms, carried her down under the sea, laid her tenderly on a beautiful bed and went back to his children. He was miserable when he walked around the white fort where he lived because he kept expecting to hear Eva's footsteps. Once he

King Lir.

thought he heard her laughing but when he
rushed towards the noise he found it was
Fionuala carrying on with Aed. He was so
disappointed he shouted at the children for

making a noise. Then he stalked out of the room and banged the door.

Fionuala was upset because their father was cross and she burst into tears. Aed said, 'We weren't doing any harm. We were just having fun. Our dad doesn't like us having fun any more. He has a face like a pig's bum!'

King Lir heard him and didn't say anything because he knew he'd been unreasonable. Fionuala was very like her mother. She had long blonde hair, big sea-green eyes, a heart-shaped face and skin like rose petals. Every time King Lir looked at her he remembered his lost wife and felt heartbroken, so he began spending long times away from home.

Fionuala was left to bring up her baby brothers. She used to cuddle them close to her while Aed stood in front of her and stretched his arms round all three of them and they'd sing together. They'd beautiful voices and all the courtiers loved listening to them.

When Fionuala was 16 years of age King Lir met Eva's sister Aefe, fell in love and took her back to live in the White Fort.

(The Tuthna De Danaan had different laws from our laws. Going to sleep for 1,000 years was thought to be unreasonable behaviour and that made King Lir free to marry Aefe without the nonsense of solicitors and courts and things. The White Fort, also called the White Fields of Armagh, was near the village of Newtownhamilton in County Armagh.)

At first the children and their stepmother were very happy, then a demon of jealously entered Aefe's heart. She thought, 'My husband loves his children more than he loves me. I want rid of them. I want his love all to myself.' She couldn't take them out into the woods and kill them because they wouldn't die. They'd just go to sleep for 1,000 years, wake up and tell everyone what had happened.

She couldn't poison them for the same reason, so she put on a face like a Lurgan spade and sat in the corner with her thumb in her mouth, doing wee smelly ones and thinking evil thoughts. She decided the best thing she could do was put a spell on them that turned them into swans.

'That's a great idea,' she muttered. 'There won't be any bodies lying about and nobody'll recognise them. I'll take them down to Lough Derravaragh to have a picnic. They like swimming. Once they're in the water I'll cast my spell. Ha! Ha! Ha! I'll make them spend 300 years on Lough Derravaragh then make them fly up to the Sea of Moyle for another 300 years before spending the last 300 years of my spell on Inis Glora in the Western Sea.

'There's a strange new religion coming to Ireland. It's called Christianity. It will change the old beliefs and cause all spells to be broken. I can't do anything about that! I won't worry about it. 900 years is probably enough for my purposes.'

Aefe waited until King Lir had gone out hunting before going to the children and saying, 'Would you like to go for a picnic? It's such a beautiful day we could ask Daire [their charioteer] to prepare the chariot with a picnic and take us along the banks of the stream that goes into the lough.

The Children of Lir.

'You love swimming, don't you? We could have a dip.'

The children rarely had the opportunity to get out of the White Fort, so they were delighted. They rushed out to the chariot and jumped in beside Aefe. Daire shook the reins and set off.

The children sang until they reached the shore, dived into the water and enjoyed splashing each other.

Aefe smiled bitterly. 'That's the last fun you'll have for nine hundred years,' she muttered softly. Her face became ugly and threatening. She stood on a rock above the lough and began to cast a spell in the old language belonging to the Formorians. They lived in Ireland before the Tuthna de Danannan arrived. She raised her wand and shrieked:

And Earth shall not hold thee,
Fire shall ye fear,
Water be thy element,
And that of Air.

A storm swirled round the lough, the water blazed with such a bright light it hurt the eyes of anyone who saw it and Daire fell to the ground.

Fionuala screamed. Her brothers appeared to be evaporating, disappearing into a white mist. A sudden agonising pain ripped through her body. She looked down. She was turning into a mist. She fainted, and when she opened her eyes she was a swan. Her brothers had also turned into swans. They snuggled close. 'What happened?' asked little Conn.

'Ha! Ha! Ha!' laughed Aefe, 'I wasn't sure if that would work! I've got rid of you. Nobody'll know what I've done. You're swans for 900 years and anyone who heard my spell will sleep for 1,000 years! Now I'll have your father's love all to myself! Ha! Ha! Ha!'

Little Conn began to cry, 'I want to go home. I love my daddy.'

'What!' shrieked Aefe, 'Do you mean to say you can still feel love? And you can still talk?'

'Yes,' replied Fionuala, 'I still love my father and you can hear me talking.'

'I don't suppose your human hearts and voices matter. You're swans and you'll be swans for 900 years. Nobody'll recognise you in your new feathered outfits. Ha! Ha! Ha!

You'll spend 300 years here, 300 years on the Northern Sea and 300 years on the Western Sea. Ha! Ha! Ha!'

She climbed into the chariot and drove off.

Fiacre and Conn started to cry, so Fionuala wrapped her wings around them and began to sing. Aed swam over, faced Fionuala and wrapped his wings around his sister and wee brothers.

Daire got up. He was shaking with rage. 'That vixen,' he said, 'deserves to have her face shoved through the back of her neck!'

The swans couldn't help laughing.

Fionuala asked, 'Why didn't the spell work on you? Why didn't you go to sleep?'

'I'm descended from kings. Evil spells don't work on me. She just knocked me down and I pretended to be asleep. Stay here and I'll go and tell your father what's happened.'

King Lir was furious with Aefe. He dragged her down to the shores of the lough and demanded she return his children to their normal shape and get out of his sight. He shouted that he never wanted to see her again.

Aefe burst into tears and tried to undo her spell, but failed.

King Lir sent for the Red Rob, the most powerful magician in the land, who did his best to break the spell. It was impossible. Red Rob turned towards the courtiers.

'Let this be a warning. Never mess with magic. Aefe's not a qualified magician. She's a certain amount of knowledge and that's a dangerous thing. She's got the spell slightly wrong. It's impossible to undo it and the poor children are doomed to be swans for 900 years.'

Red Rob flew into a rage. 'Aefe,' he guldered, 'You've committed an unforgivable crime. I hereby curse you. From hence forth you'll be without form, a pain-filled spirit in the eye of the hurricane.'

There was a sudden WSHOOSH, and Aefe gave a blood-curdling shriek and disappeared.

Conn sobbed, 'I won't be able to sleep in my own bed, I can't play hurling, I can't eat normal food.'

'That's true,' Fionuala comforted, 'but we should think positively. It could be a lot worse. Think of all the things we can do. We've still got our human hearts and voices. Let's cheer ourselves up by singing.' The others agreed so they sang ancient Irish airs and the courtiers clapped and cheered.

King Lir said, 'I hereby issue a decree that killing, or attempting to kill a swan is against the law.' (In this country it's still against the law to kill swans.)

The next 300 years passed quickly. King Lir moved his court to the banks of Lough Derravaragh. They had plenty to eat and plenty of company. They amused themselves by singing. You know the old saying, 'Use it or lose it', don't you? The opposite is true. Use it and it gets better. There's another old saying, 'Practice makes perfect'. The children's voices became more beautiful with the passing years and they attracted large and larger audiences. People throughout Ireland heard about them and they became famous, like pop stars today.

They were reasonably happy, until they felt a strange feeling pulling them towards the North. It got stronger and stronger. It was impossible to ignore.

King Lir was very upset. 'That's Aefe's spell,' he said. 'You can't escape. You'll have to go North.' They kissed him goodbye and were lifted into the air and dragged to the Sea of Moyle, which is around Ireland's north coast.

I love the north coast. That's where you can visit the Giant's Causeway, the ruins of Dunluce Castle, White Park Bay and Carrick-a-Rede Rope Bridge (a bridge, made from ropes that runs between the mainland and an island that is used by fisherman. It's scary!

Before I could stop him my son, John, ran halfway across the bridge when he was 8. He looked down and saw waves and rocks a long way below and nearly wet his pants! I had to go and rescue him and I was terrified! The secret is to keep looking ahead and not look down. Of course, Carrick-a-Rede Rope Bridge didn't exist during the lives of the Children of Lir.)

The Sea of Moyle is where icy water from the Arctic hits land. It's very, very cold. The last time I went swimming there I was 12 years of age. I went blue and shivered for half an hour afterwards and decided I was never ever doing that again! And I never have!

The children were frozen. It's no fun being a swan and having your legs and bum in cold water! To make matters worse, there was a raging gale when they arrived. They had to struggle against howling wind with towering waves crashing against over them. They became separated.

Fionuala was lucky. She was blown on to Rathlin Island. That's a beautiful place in the sea between Ireland and Scotland. (You can visit Rathlin. A ferry runs between Ballycastle and Rathlin, where you can visit a bird sanctuary during the summer months. If you're lucky you'll see lots of puffins. They are tiny cute sea birds with peculiar beaks that are brightly coloured during the mating season. The mummy puffin lays one egg and the daddy helps her hatch it. When the baby comes out of its shell it looks like a tiny cream egg!)

Fionuala found herself beside a huge cave with a large rock across its mouth. She staggered inside. It was dark and comparatively quiet. The rock kept the waves from crashing inside. She was cold, lonely, sore and covered in bruises. She curled up in the corner and cried and cried.

Next day Fionuala crept to the mouth of the cave and began to sing. Aed heard her and swam towards her voice. They hugged each other. Fionuala asked where he'd been. He said, 'On the rocks at the Giant's Causeway! I was lucky I wasn't hurt. I heard you singing and followed the sound. Let's sit on that big rock on the outside of the cave and sing. Maybe our brothers will hear us.'

They sang for hours but there was no sign of their wee brothers. Fionuala became hoarse and Aed flew up into the air to see if he could see any sign of them. He went around in a circle with his eyes scanning the horizon. Suddenly he yelled, 'Fionuala,

I see a tiny white speck! I think I it might be Conn!'

Fionuala and Aed sat outside the cave and sang louder than ever. The speck came closer. It was Conn! They rushed out to greet him and wrapped their wings round him.

Conn was so pleased to see them he burst into tears. 'I was so lonely without you,' he sobbed, 'I thought I'd have to spend the next 600 years all by myself. I was blown onto the Mull of Kintyre.'

The three children sat outside the cave and sang all day but there was no sign of Fiacre. Next day Fionuala said, 'Aed heard us singing as far away as the Mull of Kintyre. Fiacre must be hurt, or he would have heard our singing and joined us. I think he's lying somewhere and can't move. Let's go and look for him.'

They swam along Antrim's coast and searched the Skerries near what is now Portrush. Fiacre wasn't there. They looked further north. When they reached the place that is now Portstewart they heard a weak cry. They followed the sound and found Fiacre lying on the rocks. He'd a broken wing, a leg fractured in several places and he was badly bruised. He'd have been dead if he hadn't been a member of the Tuthna da Dannan.

They used their wings to lift him and carry him to Rathlin.

The next 300 years were miserable. They missed King Lir and their friends. They were lonely. The winter nights were long and dark, food was scarce and the sea made their bums numb with cold. They missed having human bodies. Conn complained, 'My feet are freezing and I can't even fart to warm them up!' (Birds aren't like us. We have an opening for wee and another one for poo. Birds only have one opening for both piddle and poo, so they do both jobs in one go and they're like spiders in that they can't fart!)

The children were delighted when they felt themselves being pulled towards the south. They didn't resist but rose high up into the air and started their long journey.

Aed, yelled, 'Yippee! That's 600 years of the curse done. We've only 300 more years before turning back into humans.'

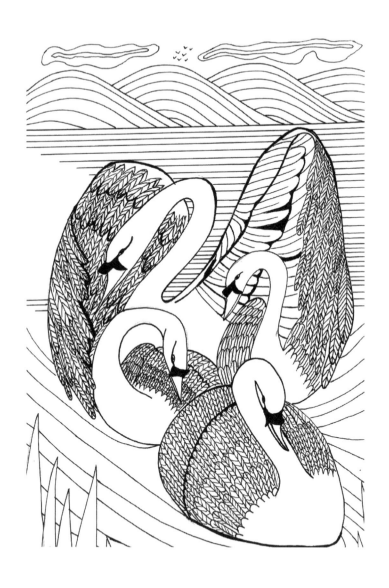

My enchanted bum's freezing!

They burst into tears as they flew over their old home because it had disappeared. There was nothing left apart from grassy banks, and Lough Derravaragh seemed smaller than they remembered. The king and his courtiers had gone for their long sleep. They'd hoped they'd be able to wave at King Lir and their friends.

Eventually they reached Inish Glora, a small island in a chain containing the larger Achill Island in the Western Sea around County Mayo.

The Western Sea is part of the Atlantic Ocean, so it's cold, although people living around that part of the world say it is surprisingly warm! They say it's influenced by the Gulf Stream, which flows towards the North along the coast. I don't believe them because I went paddling in it once and thought my feet were going to fall off with the cold! I haven't been swimming there and am not going to! All I can say is it's not quite as cold as the Sea of Moyle, and the four swans found life easier there than on Rathlin Island. There was more food and when they sang, all the birds of the air came and joined in. That was fun! Birds still enjoy singing on Inish Glora, so it's become known as 'the island of the birds'.

They had lived on Inish Glora for over 200 years when Kermock the hermit came and set up home on the shore nearby. They were glad to have company, watched him carefully and found him very interesting. Every day he went out on the shore and prayed to a strange new God. Eventually Fionuala became so curious she went up to him and said, 'What are you doing?' Kermock was so surprised he jumped, forgot he was a monk, and did a big loud one!

Fionuala said, 'Please don't be frightened. Have you ever heard of the Children of Lir?' Kermock said he'd heard an ancient tale about four children being turned into swans by a wicked spell but he hadn't paid much attention to it.

Fionuala explained that she was one of the children and introduced her brothers, and they became firm friends. Kermock gave them food and they helped him find wood to construct a strange building that looked like an upturned boat. He explained they were building one of the first Christian churches in Ireland and he was expecting a visit from a very holy man called St Patrick.

Aed asked, 'What's Christian?'

Kermock replied, 'It's a new religion. Jesus is the Christ, the Son of God. The new religion's called Christianity after Him. He came down from heaven to tell us that God loves each one of us.'

Fiacre got excited and began jumping up and down while beating his wings, 'Goody! Goody! Goody!' he yelled, 'Do you remember Aefe said we'd be released from her spell after 900 years when a new religion came to Ireland? I've lost count of time but we must have done about 900 years. We've been swans for a long time!'

Kermock asked, 'If you get your human bodies back again what's the first thing you're going to do?'

Fionuala said, 'I'm going to have a long drink of nice cold water from the spring near your church.'

The others agreed and Kermock asked, 'What's so special about drinking water from the well?'

Conn said, 'We don't know why, but we can't put our heads down, have a slug of water and swallow it. We have to pick water up with our beaks, point our heads straight up in the air and let it run down our throats. It's a nuisance.'

(He's right! Drinking is much easier for humans than birds. We could stand on our heads and drink water. I don't suggest you do that but you could bend over a stool, pick a glass of water up off the floor and see if you can drink it. You have strong muscles that can push water up your gullet (peristalsis) so you can drink it against the pull of gravity. Birds can't do that. Watch a bird having a drink. Did you see how it took a sip, then straightened its neck so its beak pointed into the air above its head and the water could run down its throat?)

The swans were happier after Kermock arrived. They grew to love him and enjoyed working with him. He loved to hear them singing and taught them strange new tunes. They grew more and more excited as the day approached for St Patrick to arrive. Eventually they spotted a boat on the horizon and watched as it drew close to shore. A man stepped out and the church bell rang for the first time.

'OOOOOOH!' spluttered Aed, 'I feel queer!'

Fionuala screamed, 'So do I!'

There was a loud BANG and a flash of lightning. Silver chains around their necks grew larger. Fiacre choked and gasped, 'I can hardly breathe.'

A splitting sound rent the air as the chains snapped and the swan plumage fell around their feet, allowing four small ancient people to step over the feathers.

Aed burst out laughing, 'Look at you Fionuala! The last time I saw you, you were a tall beautiful young girl. Now look at you! You're tiny!'

Yer man's dead on!

'What do you expect? I'm now more than 900 years old! And what makes you think you're any oil painting? You've shrunk and your beard is down past your knees! And look at Conn and Fiacre! They're not young children any more! They look ancient. The spell has been broken!'

Time passed. One morning, Kermock noticed the siblings hadn't got up. He went to see what had happened. Everything looked quiet and peaceful. He went to the door of their hut and peeped in. He thought they were sleeping but when he went closer and touched them he found they were stone cold. They'd died peacefully in their sleep. They were buried with Fionuala lying on her back and Conn and Fiacre in her arms facing her, while Aed lay on top with his arms stretched around his siblings.

Kermock said, 'I'm going to miss them, but I should be happy for them. Look at the way they are smiling. They must have gone straight to heaven and are singing in paradise.'

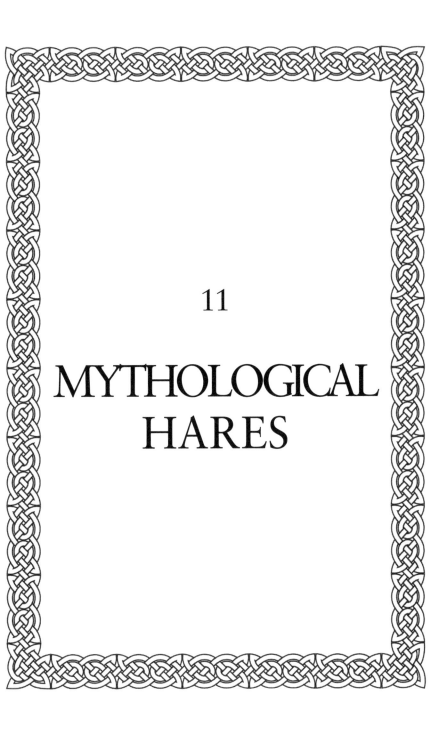

11

MYTHOLOGICAL
HARES

Whenen I was a wee girl, my mummy and daddy used to take me camping in the Sperrin Mountains. I thought they were so high, so remote and so beautiful, they must be near heaven. I pictured God sitting on his throne above me with a huge watering can at his side, and every time he wanted it to rain he picked the watering can up and watered the land below!

Now I'm grown up I know God's not sitting beside a watering can in the sky, but I still think the Sperrins are beautiful.

One day I was in Omagh when I noticed a signpost pointing to An Creâgan and thought, 'That looks interesting,' so I followed it and drove what seemed like miles along a country road through the mountains, eventually coming to a beautiful modern building set down a slight hollow. I parked my car and went inside the centre. It was fascinating.

An Creâgan is Irish for the Sperrin Centre. It has an excellent shop and cafe, interesting displays, a camp site, self-catering accommodation and friendly staff, who told me about the Creágan white hare, the song written about it and the sculpture of it that sits in their grounds:

The Creágan White Hare

In the lowlands of Creágan there lived a
    White Hare,
As swift as a swallow that flies through the air.
You may search through this world but find
    none to compare
With the pride of lower Creágan, our bonny
    white hare.

The fame of the white hare spread far and wide. Everybody wanted to capture her. The song goes on to say that one day:

There were some jolly sportsmen came here
    from Pomeroy,
Coalisland, Cookstown and likewise the Moy.
With their pedigree greyhounds they brought
    from afar
And they landed in Creágan in a fine motorcar.

The poor hare was chased up hill and down dale until eventually she was cornered and surrounded by seven men and nine dogs. She must have been terrified! But:

When she looked at the greyhounds, she raised her big ear,
She rose on her toes and with one mighty spring,
Jumped over the greyhounds and cleared through the ring.

That was some jump, wasn't it? She was so good at escaping that people thought she must be a witch, because in the past people thought witches would turn into hares and do wicked things, such as put a spell on farmers' cows so their milk couldn't be turned into butter.

One day a farmer was walking, with his dog, through his fields. He was worried because he didn't have enough money to pay his rent and if the rent wasn't paid he knew he'd be made homeless.

Yon hare must be a witch.

'I don't know what's happened to my cows,' he muttered. 'It's impossible to churn their milk into butter. If I had butter to sell I'd have all my rent money.'

A huge hare ran in front of him. He stamped his feet on the ground and said to his dog, 'Come on Nell! That hare's a witch. She's stolen our cow's milk. Let's kill her and have her for dinner.'

He chased the hare and shot at her, and hit her, but his bullet had no effect. She turned around and laughed at him. The only sort of bullet that can kill a witch is one made from silver. The farmer laughed too because he had a silver bullet in the back pocket of his trousers! He put it into his gun, shot at the hare and hit her leg. She gave a terrifying scream and ran for her life, leaving a trail of blood behind.

The farmer and his dog followed the trail, which led to a tiny cottage hidden deep in the woods. They pushed the door open and found an old woman sitting by the fire tying a bandage around her bleeding leg!

My friend Graham Mawhinney told me about the gigantic hare of Cavanreagh that was captured about the 1850s. It lived for years on land belonging to James Smyth of Cockhill and annoyed him by spending the winter eating his crop of turnips! A group of hunters decided they were going to get that hare come hell or high water. They knew local farm dogs were no match for it so they scoured the countryside looking for fast dogs and managed to find a pair of greyhounds.

The hare outpaced most of the dogs but the greyhounds kept on chasing her. She would have been running yet if she hadn't made a big mistake and dashed into a muddy field where she got stuck in the mud. One of the dogs jumped on top of her and when the hunters caught up they found the hare was dead and the dog was so exhausted it had to be put in the doggy equivalent of intensive care! An ordinary hare weighs between 7 and 8 pounds, while the Cavanreagh hare weighed 20 pounds!

In other words it was huge – but it was caught, and so it never became as famous as the Creâgan White Hare.

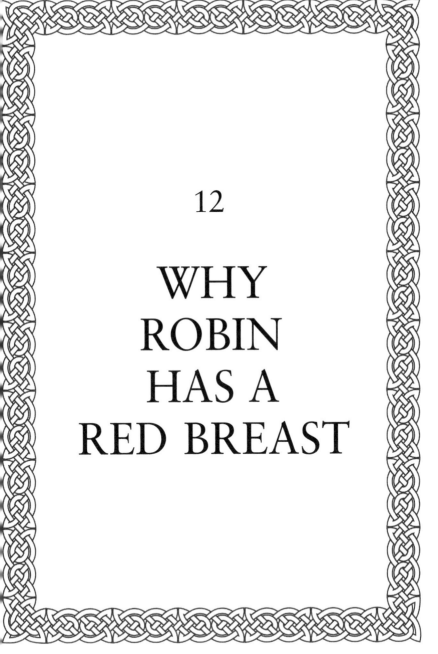

12

WHY
ROBIN
HAS A
RED BREAST

Y ou know what a robin looks like, don't you? It's the small bird with a red breast you see on Christmas cards. It's very common in gardens and it's cheeky. I had one that used to land on my spade when I was digging!

When I was wee I thought when a robin sang it was saying things like, 'it's a beautiful day', 'I'm very happy', 'listen to my song', or even 'you are my friend'. Then one day I was playing in the garden with my favourite doll, Jennifer. She was wearing a new dress granny had made her and sitting on a seat in the garden. A robin sat on a bush and sang his heart out. I thought he liked Jennifer and was singing a lovely song to her. I was very surprised when he flew down and attacked her!

I chased the robin off and told my mummy, who said, 'Robin didn't like Jennifer's red dress. Robins look cute, but they're nasty. They pick a place to live and fight any other robin who comes near. Their red breasts are warning signs that say, "Push off, or I'll fight you!" They're sensible because although they'd

Clear off or I'll knock the stuffing out of you!

fight to the death, they avoid doing that by
flashing their red breasts as a warning. If
that doesn't work, they sing loudly. The best
singer wins the battle! So if you hear a robin
singing it's really shouting insults like, 'Clear
off! Your bum's a plum!'

There's a folk tale about why a robin has
a red breast. I don't believe it, but I like it so
I'm going to share it with you. It's a nice idea.

A long time ago a robin watched a group
of soldiers roughly grab a man and nail him
to a cross. The man groaned softly. The cross

was lifted up into the air. The robin watched and was furious. 'That's a good man,' he thought. 'He's never done any harm. He's just helped people. The soldiers shouldn't be hurting him.'

Lots of soldiers and people stood around the cross and made fun of the man. The robin did his best to make them go away. He sat on a bush and sang all kinds of insults like, 'Wind yer neck in!', 'Your face is like my bum!' and 'Your head's up your backside!'

Nobody paid any attention so the robin buzzed them. Again people didn't pay any attention. The robin thought, 'Drastic action is needed. I'll dive bomb them.' He flew over the people and pooed on them! Nobody took any notice, apart from a soldier who got poo in his eye!

By this time the robin was very upset. He looked at the man and flew into a temper! 'That's ridiculous,' he fumed. 'Those brutes .have hammered thorns into the poor man's head. It looks like a crown. That must be sore. I wonder if I could pull them out.' He flew down, tried to pull the thorns out with his beak and became covered in blood.

The man, although he was in great pain, smiled and said, 'Don't worry, robin. Soon I'll be in paradise and from this day onwards you'll have a red breast.'

13

THE
MYSTERY
OF THE
BLACK
PIG'S DYKE

Ireland's counties Armagh, Cavan, Down, Leitrim, Monaghan and Longford are full of the mysterious, huge, double earthen banks with a ditch in between them that are along some of the roads. Nobody knows why they're there, what they were for or who made them. People used to think they marked borders, but that doesn't make a lot of sense. What were they bordering and why? They might once have been joined and bits of it may have been flattened. Nobody knows! They are called the Black Pig's Dyke and the longest piece is in County Longford. It stretches 6 miles (10.3km) between Lough Kinale and Lough Gowna.

There are a lot of stories about the Black Pig's Dyke. Most of them tell of a bad-tempered school teacher who had a magic wand. If his class annoyed him he'd turn them into pigs and send them out into the playground, where they frisked around all day. He changed them back into children before going-home time so their parents never knew how they'd spent the day! Perhaps the spell

School was a quare joke!

caused them to forget or maybe they enjoyed being pigs and chasing each other all day rather than having to do sums and reading so they didn't tell anyone!

My favourite Black Pig's Dyke story is about a place outside the village of Meigh, near Newry. A hill with shrubs growing on it is part of the Black Pig's Dyke. It's at a dip in the road where a bridge crosses the Flurry River.

Once upon a time, in the days before St Patrick, the village of Meigh had a school master who had the Black Art. He was very bad tempered and when he flew into a rage he used to get out his magic wand and turn his pupils into hares and hounds. That was good fun if you happened to be a hound but terrible if you were a hare! He was a mean nasty bully and he had favourites. Michael was a shy quiet wee lad some of the other boys used to bully so the master was always turning him into a hare. The poor wee lad spent his days being bitten by the hounds and he started having nightmares. Night after night he woke up screaming his head off. Eventually his father discovered what the master was doing. He was furious! Apart from anything else, he didn't like having his sleep disturbed!

Michael's father went into school, grabbed the master's wand, tapped the master with it and turned him into a gigantic pig with huge tusks. The boys laughed and laughed. The pig was raging, stuck his tusks into the ground and ran all round the countryside digging a trench that formed the Black Pig's Dyke.

14

THE
DABHUR
CHUR
MONSTER

I'm sure you've heard of the monster called Nessie that lives in Loch Ness. Do you know Ireland has its own monster? It's in Lough Ree, West Meath. Athlone, which is in the middle of Ireland, is at the northern end of the lough.

You'd wonder why few people know about Ireland's monster. Perhaps it's because of its name? Nessie sounds cute and it's easily remembered, while Ireland's monster is called the Dabhur Chur, which means 'Irish crocodile'.

There's a very old story about the monster and St Mochua, who lived a long time ago near Lough Ree. He must have been very famous because somebody wrote a book about him called *Life of St Mochua of Balla.* It says that one day St Mochua was out with some friends hunting a stag and it swam across to an island in Lough Ree. Most of his friends decided to let the stag escape. They were frightened because they'd heard a terrible monster was hidden underneath the deep waters. One of the men didn't believe the monster existed so

You look tasty.

he swam across to the island to kill the stag. He got over safely, found his prey and killed it, but when he was swimming back to his friends the monster came up from the depths and ate him!

It is said that if you were to kill the Dabhur Chur it would let out a blooding-curdling shriek as it died and its mate would come up from the bottom of the lough and kill you!

Another story tells about the Irish saint St Collumba, who crossed the Sea of Moyle. (Do you remember, that's where the Children of Lir had to hang out for 300 years?) One day he was wandering around the banks of Loch Ness when he stopped to watch a man who was swimming. Suddenly the monster appeared. The man was terrified and swam as fast as he could towards shore. The monster swam faster and faster. It was obvious it intended to have the man for dinner. The man thought he was a goner but St Columba used his spiritual powers to scare it and save the man's life. The monster was so upset it climbed out of the water and raced across to Lough Ree, where it must have laid a lot of eggs that turned into the ancestors of Ireland's Dabhur Chur.

All those stories are supposed to have happened a long time ago, so I don't think I believe them. But, and it's a big BUT, on 9.30pm on 18 May 1960 three respectable clerics, Father Quigly, Father Murray and Father Burke, were fishing on Lough Ree off Holly Point on a warm summer evening. One of them pointed towards an unusual object near the shore and shouted, 'Do you see what I see?'

It was the monster! They were so sure they'd seen it they told the Inland Fisheries Trust about it. I've written a copy of their description of it below.

There were two sections above the water; a forward section of uniform girth, stretching quite straight out of the water and inclined at the plane of the surface at about 30°, in length about 18-24 inches. The diameter of this long leading section we would estimate to be about 4 inches. At its extremity which we took to be a serpent-like head, it tapered rather abruptly to a point.

Between the leading and the following sections of this creature, there intervened about two feet of water. The second section seemed to us to be a tight, roughly semi-circular loop. This portion could have been a hump or a large knob on the back of a large body under the surface that was being propelled by flippers. As to the dimensions of this section, if a loop we should say the girth of a large fifteen pound salmon; if however, a round hump … we should put its base at about 18 inches … We would estimate the overall length of the two visible sections, measured along the surface from tip of snout to end of hump, at about 6 feet.

The movement along the water was steady. There was no apparent disturbance of the surface, so that propulsion seemed to come from a well-submerged portion of the creature. There was no undulation of its body above the water. It was cruising at a very leisurely speed, and was apparently unconcerned about our presence. We watched it moving along the surface for a period of two or three minutes in a north-easterly direction. It was going towards the shore; then it submerged gradually rather than dived, and disappeared.

The monster has been spotted in other places, so it either moves around the country from lake to lake, or there are a whole lot of them living quietly at the bottom of deep lakes in Ireland.

The Irish artist Sean Corcoran and his wife saw one in 2000 on Omey Island, a tiny tidal island off the coast of Connemara.

All I can say is, I'm not going swimming at dusk in any of Ireland's lakes in case the monster decides to surface and have me for supper!

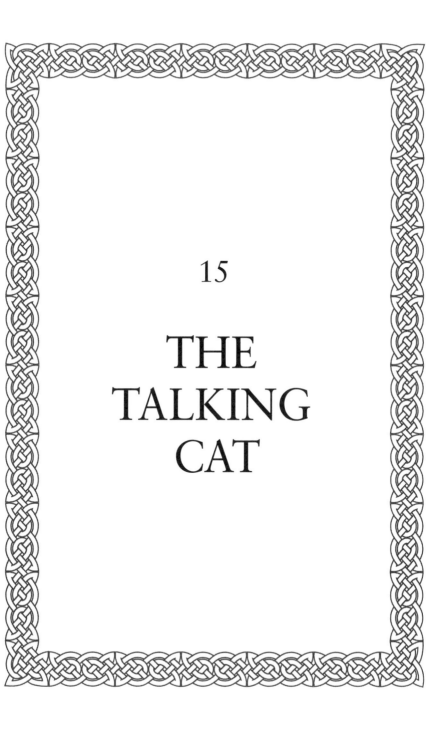

15

THE
TALKING
CAT

One day a farmer who lived in Timahoe was coming home from a fair at Portlaoise. He was very pleased with himself because he'd got a good price for his pigs, so he'd be able to pay his rent. In the old days, if you couldn't pay your rent you'd be evicted and your landowner might knock your house down.

When the farmer reached the crossroads at Money, a black cat jumped on the back of the cart. It was so heavy it caused the cart's shafts to tilt up in the air so the horse couldn't pull it.

The cat smiled and said, 'I'd like to hitch a lift.'

The farmer said, 'I'm happy to give you a lift, but only if you come up here and sit beside me. Your weight is making the shafts of the cart stick up in the air so my poor horse can't pull it.'

'Right you are,' said the cat as it moved up beside the farmer.

The cat and the farmer sat chatting until they came to the next crossroads, when the cat jumped out of the cart and shouted, 'Tell Prettyface the Booman is dead.'

When the farmer got home he put the cart away, let the horse into a field and went into the kitchen, where his wife asked him how he'd got on.

He said, 'Fine. I got a good price for the pigs and a funny thing happened on the way home. I met a talking cat.'

'Feel your head! Cats don't talk.'

'I told you, this one did.'

'You're either crazy, or you've been at the poiteen!'

'I haven't touched a drop. I'm stone-cold sober.'

'Well! I still think you're not the full shilling. From the point of view of interest, what did the cat say?'

'It said to tell Prettyface the Booman's dead!'

Prettyface was sitting dozing by the fire. She immediately jumped up and shouted, 'I must be gone or I'll be late for the funeral!' She rushed out the door and was never seen again.

Prettyface.

16

BRISTLE
AND
GRUNT

Bristle was going to see his best friend Grunt, and what could be better than going to see a good friend? He was happy, so he sang as he skipped along the narrow path in the forest with his pigs trotting behind. He loved his pigs. They were fat and well fed.

> Hey diddle-le-dee, I think I'll have a pee,
> Hey diddle-le-dum, I'll have another one!

He was pleased with life so he sang louder than ever.

> Hey diddle-le-dee, I think I'll have a pee!
> Hey diddle-le dum, I'll have another one!

He, like his friend Grunt, was a member of the Shee, that's the organisation that governs fairies. He was the strangest fairy you've ever seen; ugly, dressed in rags with his chin covered in bristles and long straggling hair. He reached the meeting place, stood in the middle of the clearing and shouted, 'GRUNT!'

There was no answer, so he looked around and thought, 'I bet Grunt's hiding.'

The only thing he could see was a fresh smelly cowpat. He looked closely. It was covered in flies. One of the flies was bigger than the rest.

'Grunt!' he yelled, 'I see you.'

The flies disappeared and an ugly old man appeared with a herd of pigs. Grunt was ugly, small like Bristle, and he had a long straggly beard and long tatty hair. He was dressed in filthy rags.

'Bristle!' he shouted, 'Well spotted. You look great!'

The two old friends hugged each other and danced around the clearing.

Then Grunt started boasting, 'I'm a great magician. The best in the land!'

Bristle was annoyed. 'You're a good magician, but I'm better than you,' he said, as he turned himself into a golden eagle.

Grunt didn't like anyone arguing with him so yelled, 'You're a jumped-up nothin! I'm a better magician that you!' He quickly turned himself into a dragon, a butterfly, an owl, a snake, a mouse, a raven and back into his normal body.

Bristle snorted, 'That ain't nothing!' He turned himself into a dog, a cat, a tiger, a lion, a rat, a vulture and then back into his own body.

'That's nothing!' shouted Grunt, turning himself into a dragonfly, a tiger, a wren, a monkey, a flea that bit Bristle, and finally into a fish, which jumped into the river before turning back into Grunt. He stood in the middle of the clearing with water dripping from him.

Bristle laughed and laughed! 'Ha! Ha! ha! Hey diddle-le-diddle, Grunt is leaking piddle!'

That made Grunt rage, so Bristle shouted it more loudly, 'Hey diddle-le-diddle, Grunt is leaking piddle!'

Grunt was cross because he was proud of being able to last all day without needing a piddle. He flew into a temper, rushed at Bristle, threw him to the ground and bit him. The two old friends began to fight. They fought day and night until they became exhausted.

Grunt quietly put a spell on Bristle's pigs so they became thinner and thinner. Bristle's employer looked at his once healthy pigs and

Ha! Ha! Ha! Look at Grunt leaking piddle!

scolded. 'You're a no-good lazy fairy. If your pigs don't look better soon, I'll sack you.'

His pigs didn't get better. They got worse and Bristle was sacked. He crept away into the darkest part of the forest, sat down and cried. 'Oh dear!' he moaned. 'I took good care of my pigs, now look at them! They look as if they're dying. What happened?'

Suddenly he realised Grunt had put a spell on them. He was furious, so he put a spell on Grunt's pigs and Grunt lost his job, too.

Grunt guessed what had happened, found Bristle and stood shaking his fists and shouting. 'My bum looks better than your face!'

They started to fight. The noise of their battle disturbed the countryside for months. Eventually, they disappeared and there was silence!

Some time later a couple of men saw two ravens fighting in County Roscommon. They watched until one said, 'Those ravens remind me of Bristle and Grunt!'

There was a sudden flash, the ravens disappeared and the two ugly old fairies appeared.

One of the men asked, 'Who are you?'

'We're Bristle and Grunt, the fairy pig herders.'

'Tell us what happened to you.'

Bristle said, 'The Shee (do you remember that's the organisation that governs fairies?) decided we would give them a bad name so they put a spell on us. We have to be animals and fight forever and ever. We'll cause wars.'

'We're sick of fighting,' sighed Bristle, 'Every time somebody spots us we have to change shape. We don't remember what we are!'

Then they changed into water animals and jumped into the River Suir.

Years later the Men from Ulster and the Men from Connaught had a party. Unfortunately they drank too much mead and began to fight. They were so drunk that fighting became impossible because they kept falling down.

Two warriors appeared and one offered to act as Champion for the North, the other for the South. They fought for three days and three nights until the effects of the drink wore off and the men joined the fight again.

News of a great war between Ulster and Connaught spread throughout Ireland, and warrior troops arrived to join the battle. Hundreds of men were killed, along with four kings.

The battle raged until the men became fed up and realised their champions were Bristle and Grunt.

The Men of Ulster crept back over the border to Slieve-na-man. (That's a mountain in South Armagh. Its name means 'Mountain of the Women'.) Bristle and Grunt turned into two huge shadows who jumped out on people, scared them and caused them to wet themselves, or die of fright.

Eventually they tried to scare an old woman who was walking past a graveyard by leaping out from behind the wall and screaming.

She was so old she was ready to die, so she laughed! 'Ha! Ha! Ha! You don't scare me! You're Bristle and Grunt! Ha! Ha! Ha! May the fleas of a thousand donkeys jump on your bums and may your arms become too short to scratch!' She laughed and laughed until tears ran down her cheeks.

Bristle and Grunt were ashamed. They felt they'd made fools of themselves. They turned into eels and disappeared.

Bristle travelled as an eel to a spring in County Connaught, where he met nasty Queen Maeve. (She was so posh she had a slave to wipe her bottom after she did a poo! Once, when she was fighting a battle with Cuculan, she got caught short and disappeared behind a bush and did such a big piddle and poo the place is called 'The Place Of Queen Maeve's Foul Deed!' It's up Knocknaree Mountain. Do you remember Cuculan and Queen Maeve from the story about the Murderous Morrigan?) Bristle was swallowed by one of her cows and reborn as a beautiful white calf, which grew into the finest white bull in the whole of Ireland.

The white bull didn't like Queen Maeve, so he went to live with her husband. She was very annoyed! She wanted a prize-winning bull, so she gathered an army and marched on Ulster to steal a brown bull belonging to a chieftain called Dara. She didn't know, but that big brown bull was really Grunt! He'd gone into the River Cronn on the Cooley Peninsula, where he was swallowed by one of the Dara's cows. It gave birth to a brown calf, which became the finest brown bull in the whole of Ireland. Grunt was sick of fighting so he became an unusually good-tempered bull. He was huge. Two hundred men of Ulster could sleep in his shadow. He sang to them at night and allowed children to play on his back.

Dara lived on at Dulargy. (The remains of his home are still there and may be seen if you drive towards Carlingford, go past the Ballymascallon Hotel and take the road on the left towards Dulargy. Look for a mound on the right side of the road a short distance from the main road to Carlingford. A modern bungalow has been built into it, but you can still make out the ancient remains of Dara's old dwelling place.)

When Dara heard Queen Maeve intended to steal Grunt he hid him in a stockade behind what is now Ravensdene School and gave him nine cows to keep him company. Grunt enjoyed talking to the girls and sleeping in the sun, until the Morrigan saw him and shouted, 'Look at you! You big soft edjiot! What do you think you are? A pussycat? You should be ashamed of yourself! Ulster's being attacked and what are you doing? Lazing around enjoying yourself! Remember you're a bull, move your bum. Get up and FIGHT!'

Grunt was annoyed. He jumped up, shook the children off his back, pawed the ground,

Do you think you're a pussy cat?
Get out there and fight!

broke out of the stockade and headed south. When the brown bull met the white bull they fought and fought. The brown bull killed the white bull, but he was badly hurt. He managed to stagger home before his great heart gave out but he dropped dead near Banbridge and that was the end of Bristle and Grunt.